MY SECRET ADMIRER

MY SECRET ADMIRER

by Stephen Roos

illustrated by Carol Newsom

A YEARLING BOOK

Published by
Dell Publishing Co., Inc.
1 Dag Hammarskjold Plaza
New York, New York 10017

For Jane Eager

Yearling ® TM 913705, Dell Publishing Co., Inc.

ISBN: 0-440-45950-8

Reprinted by arrangement with Delacorte Press
Printed in the United States of America
First Yearling printing—September 1985

CW

AUTHOR'S NOTE

Readers of *My Horrible Secret* and *The Terrible Truth* know that made-up names were used to protect the identity of the parties involved. Certain individuals have asked that this policy be continued and the author is happy to oblige.

Contents

Chapter One

I ♥ New Eden

Claire Van Kemp looked at her watch again and sighed. It was already two fifty-one. If Mrs. Simkins didn't hurry up with the Civil War, there wouldn't be any time left for class discussion. Claire adjusted her glasses and tried to sit quietly at her desk in the last row of the classroom. Of all the virtues, patience was the one she was worst at. Sometimes she even wondered who had decided it was a virtue in the first place.

"Your homework assignment for tonight is to read Lincoln's Gettysburg Address, on page two-oh-six," Mrs. Simkins said. "We're going to have a quiz on it at the end of the week."

Mrs. Simkins gave the map at the front of the classroom a tug and it snapped up to its roller. Claire shot her hand into the air.

"If you shake your hand any harder, Claire,"

Mrs. Simkins said, "it's going to fall off. Is there something you don't understand about the Civil War?"

"Oh, no, Mrs. Simkins," Claire said. "It's just that I have a very important announcement to make."

Several heads in front of Claire turned around. Although it was hardly the first time that Claire had had something to announce, today she had put extra energy into her voice.

"I think we have time," Mrs. Simkins said. "Go ahead, Claire."

"A week from Friday, the Junior Chamber of Commerce is launching the first ever 'I Love New Eden' campaign," Claire said proudly. "My uncle Horace says we're all welcome to help out."

"But that's Valentine's Day," Shirley Garfield said.

"That's exactly why they're launching it then," Claire explained. "The Jaycees are setting up a booth near the train station with a great big heart on it."

"Are they having a party?" Shirley asked.

"No, Shirley," Claire said. "They'll be handing out bumper stickers. It's supposed to help tourism."

"I think we ought to have a party," Shirley said. "Just the way the kids in the high school do."

"If the party is going to be indoors, I'll

come," Randy Pratt said. "Who wants to stand in the cold handing out bumper stickers?"

"But it's important," Claire said. "We can have a party anytime."

"Not a Valentine's party," Shirley said. "You can have them only once a year."

"Tourism is vital to our community," Claire said. "That's what my uncle says."

"Parties teach us how to act on a social level," Shirley said. "That's important too."

"Are we going to have ice cream and cake?" Randy asked. "They're not just important. They're essential."

"It wouldn't be a party without ice cream and cake," Shirley said.

"Hey, wait a minute," Claire said as she jumped to her feet. "We were talking about the 'I Love New Eden' campaign."

"I thought we were talking about our Valentine's Day party," Shirley said. "We could decorate the cafeteria with lots of red streamers and tape a lot of hearts to the walls too."

"That sounds very nice," Mrs. Simkins said.

"We'll volunteer for that detail," Gracie Arnold announced.

"We?" Mrs. Simkins asked.

"You know, Margie and Kimberly and me," Gracie said. "The three of us could cut out hundreds of hearts and make the cafeteria look like a romantic fantasy."

From every corner of the classroom Claire heard ooh's and aah's. It was enough to make her sit down.

"Do you think you could save a couple dozen of those hearts for the love bin?" Shirley asked.

Claire didn't think she could stand it for another minute. A love bin, whatever that was, had to be something really horrible. "What's a love bin?" she asked, rising to her feet again.

"It's my own original idea," Shirley said. "We could find the biggest garbage can around and glue hearts all over it."

"But what's it for?" Claire asked nervously.

"For valentines," Shirley said. "We can't have a Valentine's party without them. Maybe you could borrow a garbage can from your uncle's hardware store."

"So far as I know, Uncle Horace isn't into romantic fantasies," Claire said. "He's a businessman."

"And now that you've got Van Kemperama, you're a businesswoman," Shirley said.

"So what?"

"So you're just not as interested in some things that the rest of us are interested in," Shirley explained.

"Like parties?" Claire asked.

"And *other* things," Shirley said.

Some of the other girls in the classroom smiled knowingly. A few even giggled a little.

Claire just shrugged. Ever since the beginning of sixth grade, the other things Shirley was interested in were her hair, her clothes, and boys. Claire couldn't believe that the others were letting that happen to them too.

"I think we ought to put it to a vote," Claire said. "Everyone who wants to help out the Jaycees' 'I Love New Eden' campaign instead of going to some dumb Valentine's Day party, raise your hand."

Claire looked around the classroom. In one corner she saw Gracie Arnold sitting at her desk with her hands folded. In another corner Kimberly Horowitz and Margie Neustadt were doing the same thing. So were all the other girls.

Claire looked at the boys. None of them had his hand in the air, either.

In fact, only one student had her hand up. Claire.

What was happening to everyone? Claire wondered.

"You won't forget to ask your uncle about the garbage can, will you?" Shirley asked.

Before Claire could say a word, the final bell rang. In less than a second all the kids were on their feet, shoving pads and pens into their book bags and heading for the closet. Only Claire had a briefcase. She put her textbooks into it and followed the others to the closet. She put on her red cap that came down over her straight black hair, her brown boots that came up to the knees of her jeans, her quilted down coat, and her red mittens. Then she wrapped the long red scarf around her neck and walked into the corridor.

Shirley was already standing at the main entrance. As usual, she was giggling with Gaylord Adamson and Greg Stockard.

"Hi, Claire," Greg said as she approached.

"Hi, Greg," Claire said. "Hi, Gaylord."

"Oh, Claire," Shirley said. "I hope there aren't any hard feelings about the 'I Love New Eden' campaign. We're going down to the Hot Shoppe to make plans for the party. Would you like to come?"

"Sorry," Claire said. "I can't be late for my job."

"I'm sure your uncle won't mind just this once," Shirley said.

"Business is business," Claire said.

"Then I'll just have to have two handsome escorts all to myself," Shirley said. "I hope you boys don't mind."

"Gosh, no," said Gaylord.

"Fine by me," said Greg.

Claire walked briskly down the steps to the school bus. When she got to work that afternoon, she would have to tell Uncle Horace that not one of the kids in her class had volunteered to work at the "I Love New Eden" booth. For the life of her, though, she wouldn't be able to explain why all of them wanted to go to a Valentine's party instead.

Were all the boys going girl-crazy? she wondered. Were all the girls boy-crazy? Claire shook her head. Nothing as silly as that was ever going to happen to her, she knew.

Not even in her wildest dreams.

Chapter Two

The Only Games in Town

Claire could only thank her lucky stars that she was never going to let anything like being boy-crazy sidetrack her from all the important things there were for her to accomplish in this world. Not that she had anything in particular against boys. Even if she wasn't about to go crazy over them, she would have been the first to admit that a lot of the grown-ups she admired most had been boys themselves once upon a time.

Claire's father, for instance. For as long as anyone in New Eden could remember, he had been the first selectman, which was very much like being mayor, except that New Eden was too small to have a mayor. If Claire's father weren't so admirable, he wouldn't have kept on getting re-elected over and over again.

She also admired the governor of the state. The summer before, when Claire had won the

Junior Achievement Award, she had met the governor and had lunch with him. He had spoken to Claire about setting up a list of priorities. This year, Van Kemperama was Claire's number-one priority.

Technically speaking, Van Kemperama belonged to her uncle Horace, because it was located at one end of his hardware store, but it wouldn't have come into existence if Claire hadn't thought up the whole thing in the first place.

When Claire and her parents had gone on a trip the year before, she noticed video game parlors in practically every town and city they visited. When she got back to New Eden, she noticed that almost every magazine and television show had something to do with video games. Still, it had taken until Thanksgiving for Claire to realize that it was the perfect time for New Eden to get a video game parlor of its own.

She had been wandering around the town one afternoon just as winter was setting in. With nothing much to do, she decided to stop by the hardware store. Since it was that in-between time of year when it was too late to buy rakes and too early to buy snow shovels, business at Van Kemp Hardware was slow. Uncle Horace was sitting behind the counter figuring out receipts.

"Hi there, Claire," Uncle Horace had said.

"Come on in. We're having a sale on leaf-catchers."

"I'm just looking, I guess." She started to walk up one aisle and down the next. Ever since Claire could remember, she had been fascinated by all the gadgets in Uncle Horace's store. But today it seemed to her that part of the store was missing. While two thirds of the place was crammed with paints and hammers and buzz saws, one third had nothing in it.

"How come there's nothing here, Uncle Horace?" Claire asked.

"That's where we kept the lawn mowers."

"So this whole space is going to be empty till next spring?" Claire asked. "No snowblowers, even?"

"I'm afraid not," Uncle Horace said. "We're moving all that stuff over to one of Harry's gas stations. We're going to turn it into one of those lawn-and-garden centers, you know."

Harry was the youngest of the Van Kemp brothers, which made him Claire's other uncle. He owned New Eden's two gas stations.

"Well, I don't mean to be critical," Claire said. "But is it good business sense to have so much of your store underutilized?" Underutilized was a recent addition to Claire's vocabulary, and she liked to use it whenever she could.

"You have a point there, Claire," Uncle Horace said. "Trouble is, I just don't know how to fill the space. I like to make money as much as the next businessman, but I just can't seem to come up with something surefire."

"Video games," she said.

"Video games?"

"You know," Claire said. "Like Pac-Man and Donkey Kong. They're computer games and they cost a quarter to play and everyone loves them. Kids my age especially."

"I know what video games are," Uncle Horace said. "I just don't see what they have to do with Van Kemp Hardware."

"Turn that empty part of the store into a video game parlor and you'll be a rich man."

Uncle Horace put the index finger of his right hand to his cheek, the way he always did when he was thinking. "I don't see it," he said. "Computer games aren't hardware."

"They're the hardware of the future, Uncle Horace," Claire said. "Think of it. You'll have the first hardware store in all of New Eden to move into the twenty-first century."

"Claire," Uncle Horace said. "Van Kemp's is the only hardware store in town. Even without computer games, I'm going to be the first hardware store around here that moves into *any* century that happens to come along."

"But think of the money," Claire said. "You could fit twenty games in that space. Kids spend a quarter every three or four minutes on the games."

"Well, I'll give it some thought," Uncle Horace said. "It'd mean a lot of extra work, though. I'd probably have to hire someone."

"But not full-time," Claire said. "The video arcades are busy only when school is out. You'd just need someone for a few hours in the afternoon."

"Well, where am I going to find someone who is responsible, reliable, and only wants to work part-time?"

"I can think of someone who fits the bill," Claire said. "She comes highly recommended too. In fact, only this past summer she won her first Junior Achievement Award."

Uncle Horace smiled. "Well, this person has to be awfully bright too," he said.

"As a matter of fact, Uncle Horace, this person is extremely intelligent," Claire said. "I'll show you her last report card if you like. All *A*'s."

"All *A*'s?" Uncle Horace asked. "It's hard to believe that anyone in New Eden has all these qualifications."

"Plus she works cheap," Claire said. "She'll take the minimum wage."

"She sounds too good to be true," Uncle Horace said.

"I know how you feel," Claire said. "But take my word for it."

When Claire got home that night, her father was sitting in the big chair in the den, reading his newspaper.

"Guess what, Dad?" she asked as she ran toward him. "I'm going into business with Uncle Horace. I'll be managing a video game parlor."

Mr. Van Kemp removed his glasses and rested them on his knee. "Hold on a second, Claire," he said. "When did all this come about?"

"Just this afternoon," Claire said. "It's my new project."

"But a job," her father said. "Aren't you a little young for a real job?"

"Don't worry, Dad," Claire said. "It's just afternoons. I won't even have to quit school."

"Well, that's a relief," Mr. Van Kemp said. "But there are laws around here about kids working."

"It's against the law for a kid to work?" Claire asked.

"Nothing like that," her father said. "You need to get your working papers at school and fill them out. You'll need some signatures too."

"Like yours?"

"Yes, but don't worry," her father said. "I wouldn't dream of standing in your way of making a million dollars."

"I'm not going to become a millionaire right away," Claire said. "Right now I'm trying to develop my leadership potential."

"From what I hear, your leadership potential is doing fine," Mr. Van Kemp said.

"You can't have too much of a good thing, Dad," she said. "I'm going to go tell Mom now."

As Claire left the den, her father picked up his paper and put on his glasses. When she looked back at him from the door, she saw that he was smiling.

Three days later Claire arrived at the hardware store with her working papers and introduced herself to Uncle Horace as the new manager of the future video arcade. Uncle Horace shook her hand. "Welcome, partner," he said.

Business began after New Year's when a large van had pulled up in front of Van Kemp's and unloaded ten video games, which Uncle Horace had rented from a big distributor in Boston. While Uncle Horace hooked them up, Claire made a sign that read VAN KEMPERAMA and put it up at one end of the store. The next day had been their official opening, and from the start business boomed. It seemed that every kid in town who had a quarter spent it at Van Kemperama. From the time school let out until dinnertime, the video game parlor was filled with teenagers and grown-ups, but mostly with kids from New Eden Middle School. On Saturdays the place was packed from noon on.

For almost anyone else, managing Van

Kemperama would have been a lot of work. But Claire didn't see it that way. Keeping the place tidy, taking the place of the money-changing machine when it was out of order, and showing the kids how to play the games was usually a lot of fun. As Claire walked in that afternoon in February, she saw that little Milton Marango was her first customer of the day.

How did he do it? Although Claire got there as fast as she could, little Milton was always there before she was.

"Eight thousand points," Milton yelled as soon as he saw her. "Pretty good, huh?"

"Pretty good," Claire said. "Might even be a record."

"Gosh, no," Milton said. "The record is nine thousand, three hundred and eighty points. I scored that yesterday before I went home."

"Well, don't get discouraged," Claire said. "I'm sure you'll hit your stride again."

"Can you give me change for a dollar?" Milton asked.

"Is the money-changing machine out of order again?" Claire asked.

"I don't know," Milton said. "I didn't look. It's just a lot more fun when you make the change."

That was Milton for you, Claire thought. Always underfoot. Didn't he realize that at any minute she would have to deal with an onslaught of other kids? Didn't he understand that he wasn't her only customer?

Claire reached into the pocket of her jeans and pulled out four quarters. Customer relations were important, and that meant she had to accommodate every single customer, including nerdy fifth-graders like Milton.

"When are you going to get some harder games?" Milton asked.

"These are the hardest games around, Milton," Claire said patiently.

"You've got to be kidding," Milton said. "You *are* kidding, aren't you?"

Claire hoped that her smile disguised her irritation. If it wasn't one thing with Milton, it was another. "Uncle Horace checked with the distributor last week," she said. "Video games don't come any harder than these. When there is a harder game, we'll get it. You're just going to have to wait for technology to catch up with you, Milton."

Claire knew that she could increase the skill level of the games, but that would make them too difficult for most of the other kids.

"I just hope I don't have to wait so long that my mind starts to rot," Milton said.

"In that case," Claire said, "why don't you invent a video game of your own?"

"Do you think I could?"

"Sure," Claire said. "Don't let a little thing

like being ten years old stand in your way. In the meantime, why don't you go back to Donkey Kong? The next game is on the house."

Claire held out another quarter. To her relief, Milton took it and walked over to the game.

If there had been time, Claire's sigh of relief would have been a major one. But a stream of kids was parading into Van Kemperama. Claire's workday was once again in full swing.

Not that she minded. At this rate, Claire would have her second Junior Achievement Award in the bag. Just the thought of winning it made her smile. In no time at all she forgot all about Milton, Shirley Garfield's Valentine's Day party, and Uncle Horace's garbage can.

Chapter Three

Love Bins and Garbage Cans

"I'm so excited," Gracie Arnold said breathlessly as she set her tray across the cafeteria table from Claire.

Claire took a bite of her cream-cheese-and-jelly sandwich and tried to imagine what Gracie was talking about. Before she could come up with an answer, Margie Neustadt had plunked her tray down next to Claire and Kimberly Horowitz had taken the seat next to Gracie. The three spent so much time together that they were known as "the musketeers."

"Did your uncle say it was okay?" Kimberly asked.

"About what?" Claire asked cautiously as she realized that all three of the girls were staring very intently at her.

"About the love bin," Margie said.

"We have our hearts ready for it," Gracie

said. "We dropped them off at Shirley's house yesterday afternoon."

"The love bin?" Claire asked. "You mean the garbage can? Is that what you're all so excited about?"

"Of course," Gracie said.

"Who isn't?" asked Margie.

"What else?" asked Kimberly.

"Certainly, girls," Claire said. Saying that she had forgotten all about it might cause triple heart attacks. "When does Shirley need it?"

"A couple of days before the party," Gracie said.

"Well, that leaves plenty of time," Claire said.

"No, it doesn't," Kimberly said. "Today is a couple of days before the party."

"It's the day after tomorrow?" Claire asked. "Does Valentine's Day fall on the fourteenth this year? Why didn't someone tell me?"

"It falls on the fourteenth every year," Gracie said. "It's like Christmas."

"Only better," said Margie.

"And the love bin's the best part of the whole party," Kimberly said. "You're supposed to bring it over to Shirley's house tonight."

"So she can decorate it," Margie said.

Claire leaned back in her chair and ate the last bite of her sandwich. "I don't know how I ever got involved in this love bin business in the first place," she said. "What's the big deal about Valentine's Day anyway?"

"Truthfully," Gracie said, lowering her voice a little bit, "that's how we used to feel."

"We said what's the big deal too," Kimberly said.

"But only at first," Margie said. "Until Shirley explained it to us."

"And what did Shirley have to say?" Claire asked.

"She said it was a question of maturity," Gracie said.

"I mean, we *are* sixth-graders, aren't we?" Margie said.

"Shirley had to tell you what grade you're in?" Claire asked.

"Shirley just reminded us that it was about time we started getting interested," Gracie said.

"Interested in what?" Claire asked.

The three girls looked at one another and giggled.

"Oh, come on, Claire," Margie said.

"Boys," Gracie said. "The earlier you get interested in boys, the earlier you mature. That's how life works."

"And you guys fell for it?" Claire asked.

"Shirley knows what she's talking about," Margie said. "You should hear what else she has to say on the subject. She's very informative."

Claire pushed her chair back and stood up.

She lifted her tray. "It looks like I'm going to have to give Shirley a good talking-to," she said. "Tonight. Before all this nonsense gets out of control."

"Tonight when you deliver the love bin?" Kimberly asked.

"Tonight when I deliver the garbage can," Claire announced as she threw her rubbish away and walked toward the door.

That evening after the last customer had left Van Kemperama, Claire carried the garbage can out of Uncle Horace's hardware store and dragged it along Main Street. When she got to the corner of Elm, she laid it on its side in the snow and rolled it in the direction of Shirley's house. Guiding it very gently with the toes of her boots, Claire turned in at 304 Elm and rolled it up the walk.

She set the garbage can upright and knocked on the door. A moment later Shirley was standing in front of her.

"Oh, Claire," Shirley said. "It's just beautiful."

Claire took another look. "It looks like any other garbage can to me," she said.

"Well, I was looking at it for its potential," Shirley said. "It's going to make a perfectly charming love bin."

Together they carried the garbage can into

the front hall. As Claire looked around the living room, she hardly recognized it. Everyone in town knew that Shirley's mother was the tidiest homemaker in New Eden. But tonight the Garfields' living room was a complete mess. At one end were piles and piles of the musketeers' valentines. In front of the fireplace were stacks of red and white crepe paper and rolls of Scotch tape and scissors. The coffee table was littered with cards and envelopes and red felt-tip pens.

"You know how it is when you're planning a party," Shirley said as she led Claire toward the sofa.

"I bet your mother's going to be furious when she sees this," Claire said.

"It's been like this for three days," Shirley said. "Mom understands, but she says she'll be relieved when Valentine's Day is over. I'm going to decorate the bin tonight, and tomorrow we're taking everything over to the school. Except for my valentines."

"Well, your valentines can't take up much space," Claire said.

"My valentines do," Shirley said. "They're also going to take up a lot of time. All tomorrow evening, probably. That's why I want to finish the bin tonight."

Claire looked down at the coffee table and the valentines that were spread across it. "How many valentines are you sending?" she asked.

"Well, I was thinking about sending only two or three," Shirley said. "Gaylord, of course, and Greg and Warren. Then I thought it might be awkward to single out those three. So I decided to send out a few more. To Arthur definitely. And Vincent Jefferson and Hal Rilling. But then I thought that if I sent out that many, it might hurt the feelings of all the others who weren't getting one. Boys can be very sensitive about valentines. You know, pretending they don't care and then getting all upset when they don't get one."

"So what did you finally decide to do?" Claire asked.

"I had to compromise," Shirley said. "My mother said it was the only way."

"What's the compromise?"

"I'm sending valentines to every one of the boys," Shirley said proudly.

"In the whole school?"

"Oh, not to the fourth- and fifth-graders," Shirley said. "I would never send a valentine to anyone younger. Just to all the boys in the sixth grade."

"That's going to cost you a small fortune."

"It did take up two weeks allowance," Shirley said. "But I don't mind. I see it as an investment in my future."

"The day after tomorrow, Valentine's Day will be a thing of the past," Claire said. "There's no future in valentines, Shirley."

"It's only over for a year," Shirley said. "From now on we'll be having Valentine's Day parties every year."

"It's still a long time to wait for a return on your investment," Claire said. "It doesn't sound like good business sense to me."

"Maybe I won't have to wait a whole year," Shirley said.

"I bet you will," Claire said.

"Why?"

"Because the boys in the sixth grade won't know you sent them valentines until it's too late for them to send you one in return," Claire said. "That's why."

"That isn't why," Shirley said. "The boys already know I'm sending them valentines."

"You told them?"

"My mother said telling them was the best way," Shirley said.

"You mean you went up to every boy in the class and told them you were sending them a valentine and you hoped they'd send you one too?"

"You have to be more subtle than that with boys, Claire," Shirley said. "I'd just say something like 'Gee, I hope you enjoy the valentine I picked out especially for you.' I think they got the message. How many are you sending out, Claire?"

"None," Claire said.

Shirley looked horrified. "But you've got to

send valentines," she said. "It'll be terrible if you don't. You'll feel left out. You don't want that, do you?"

"I'll take my chances," Claire said. "Some of us just aren't as romantically inclined as you are, Shirley."

"And some of us just aren't maturing as fast, either," she said. "Don't feel bad, Claire. I'm sure you'll catch up in time."

Claire felt the blood rush to her face. "Look, Shirley," she said. "You can pull that maturity bit on the musketeers, but you can't pull it on me. Valentines have nothing to do with being mature."

"It depends on how you look at it," Shirley said sweetly. "Maybe you're just afraid of boys. It's perfectly natural when you're young."

"Afraid of boys?" Claire asked. "I've never heard anything so silly in my whole life. Except for your Valentine's Day party, of course."

"Please, Claire," Shirley said. "Try to calm yourself. If you want to be unpopular, I understand."

"I'm not afraid of boys," Claire said. "And I'm not unpopular, either."

"Well, I guess we'll find out soon enough, won't we?" Shirley said.

"I guess we will," Claire said. "I bet I'll get a lot of cards. Just as many as you do. Maybe even more."

Before Shirley could utter one more word, Claire was on her feet. She stomped out of the house and slammed the front door behind her. If it was the last thing she did, she was going to show Shirley Garfield that she wasn't afraid of sending valentines.

The next afternoon Claire took time off from her job to go over to the Book Worm, the stationery and book store that everyone in town called the Worm. Since there were fourteen boys in her class, Claire bought the first fourteen valentines she saw.

At home that night she put the envelopes out on one side of her desk and put the cards on the other. Valentines were supposed to be signed "love," but as far as Claire was concerned that was far easier said than written. But she couldn't sign them just "Claire," and it couldn't be "fondly" or "affectionately." Those words were for aunts and grandmothers.

So "Love, Claire" it was. Each time she wrote it, a little wave of anxiety ran through her. What if none of the boys in the class was sending her a card? Claire felt her heart sink a little. How had she got herself into this situation?

She stuck the end of her felt-tip pen in her mouth and thought for a moment. It wasn't like Claire to admit defeat. She thought some more. Suddenly the perfect solution came to her. Without a moment's hesitation, she addressed each envelope. Then she stuffed the valentines into the envelopes, sealed them, and put them all in a neat little pile.

On Valentine's Day Claire wasn't going to worry one bit about not getting any cards. Every single one of her envelopes was addressed to Claire Van Kemp.

Chapter Four

Love, Claire

The next morning, as Claire transferred her pile of valentines from her desk to her briefcase, she realized that she was going to enjoy the day even more than she could have ever predicted. By the end of the day she would have received as many if not more valentines than anyone else in the sixth grade. They didn't call her an overachiever for nothing.

When the school bus stopped in front of New Eden Middle, Claire was first off. Quickly she made her way ahead of the others through the main hall to the large red and white bin outside the principal's office. She opened her briefcase and dropped all fourteen envelopes into the bin.

All day the students at New Eden Middle had a hard time keeping their minds on their work. When it was time for the party, everyone raced to the cafeteria.

The musketeers stood at one end of the room. They were wringing their hands and smiling bravely as though they were in some sort of contest. At the other end of the lunchroom were most of the boys, Gaylord and Warren and Greg and Arthur among them, trying to look as though they couldn't have cared less about Valentine's Day. In other parts of the cafeteria were clusters of fourth- and fifth-graders. Like the sixth-graders, most of them were divided into boy groups and girl groups.

As the women who worked in the cafeteria were putting out the cake and ice cream, Shirley dragged in the Valentine's Day bin and set it down in the center of the room.

"Shirley has been very kind to offer to distribute the valentines," Mrs. Simkins said. "But since there are so many of them, I hope others will offer to help."

The musketeers raised their hands and walked over to the bin.

"Thank you, girls," Mrs. Simkins said. "I think four will be enough unless somebody else wants to help."

Claire usually volunteered, but this time she decided against it. It would be more impressive if someone else handed her her valentines.

The four girls dug into the bin and began to pull out the envelopes.

"Here's one for Gaylord," Shirley said. "Oh,

and here's one for me." Shirley beamed and handed Gaylord his valentine and stuffed her own into her red purse.

"Here's one for Warren," Margie said.

"This one's for Marcie Lewis," Gracie said.

"And here's one for Claire Van Kemp," Kimberly said.

As Shirley, Gracie, and Margie called out the names, Kimberly handed the envelope to Claire. Claire checked the handwriting. It was hers.

"Aren't you going to open it?" Kimberly asked.

Since Claire knew exactly what was inside, she had not considered that possibility. "I was thinking of opening them when I get home."

Kimberly looked shocked. "I don't know how you can stand the suspense, Claire," she said. "Aren't you dying to find out who's sent you a valentine?"

"I wouldn't go *that* far," Claire said.

"Not even a little curious?" Kimberly teased.

Claire realized that it was going to look very odd if she refused to open her envelopes, especially when all the other kids were ripping theirs open the moment they received them.

"Well, I guess I am kind of curious," she said.

"So open it," Kimberly said.

Claire opened the envelope and pulled out the valentine.

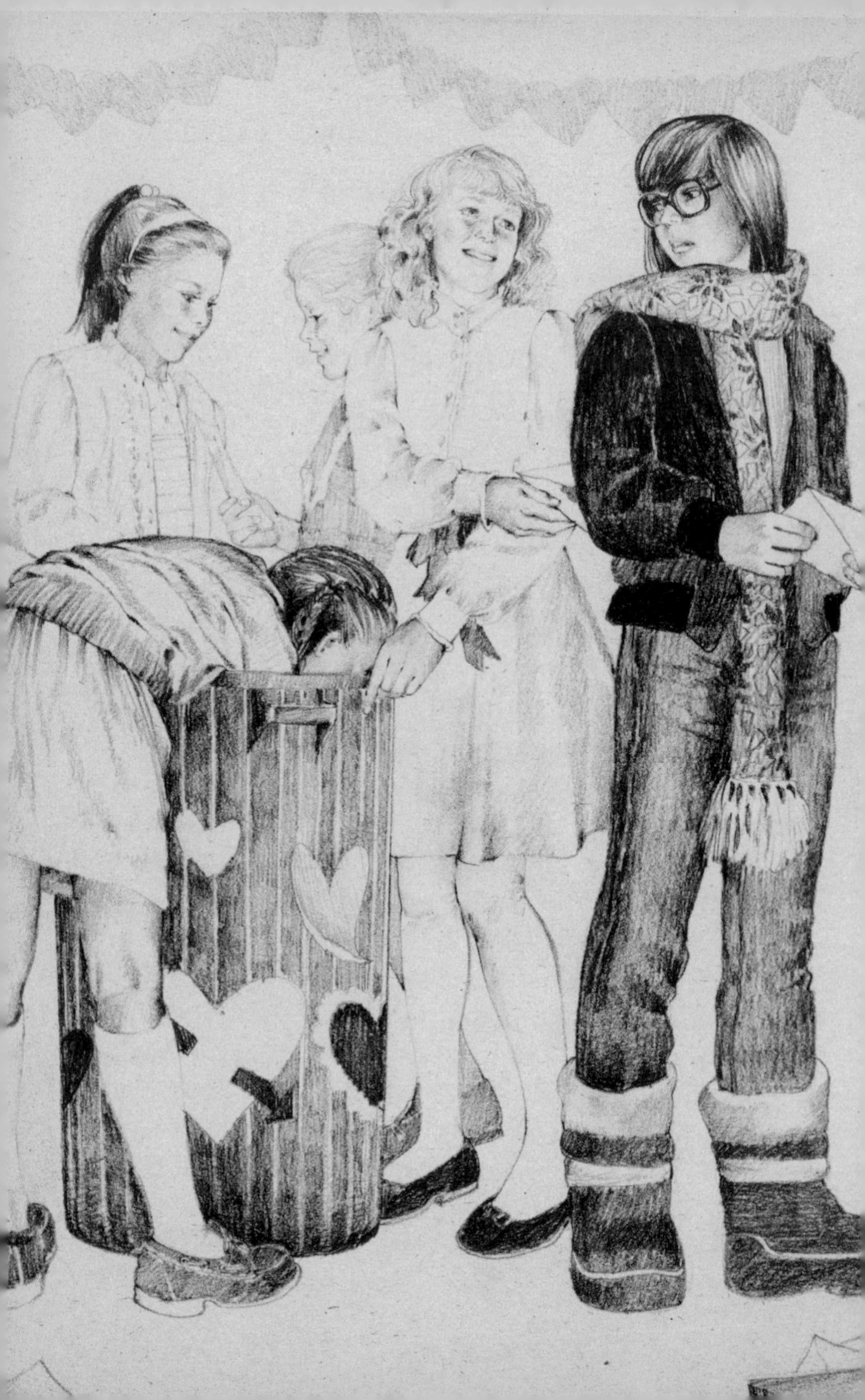

"It's very pretty," Kimberly said. "Aren't you going to see who it's from?"

Very quickly, so that Kimberly couldn't see, Claire opened the card. Just as quickly she closed it and put it back in the envelope.

"So who's it from?"

"I don't have to tell, do I?"

"Well, I'll tell you who I get valentines from if you'll tell me who yours are from," Kimberly said. "Margie and Gracie and I promised we'd tell each other, so there's no reason why we won't tell you, Claire."

"I don't happen to think that's such a great idea."

"But that's part of the fun."

"Well, maybe," Claire allowed. "But not as far as I'm concerned. Valentines can be extremely personal, don't you think?"

"Well," Kimberly said. "I didn't mean to pry."

She looked slightly offended.

"Oh, I wasn't suggesting you were prying," Claire said. "It's just that I'm kind of sensitive that way."

Kimberly looked a little less offended. She went back to the bin for more envelopes. Claire decided to step back to the outer fringe of the circle of boys and girls surrounding the bin. Only when Shirley or a musketeer called out her name did Claire step forward. She would clutch the new envelope and then step back very quickly. Just in case someone happened to be looking at her, Claire opened each envelope as she received it. She would pretend to read it, fake a little smile, and put the valentine back into the envelope.

Because there were so many envelopes, it took almost half an hour before Claire collected her fourteen.

When the last valentine was handed to her, Claire decided to get some ice cream and cake. Since she wasn't going to get any more, there was no reason for her to stand around the bin any longer. That was when she realized that she wasn't feeling as elated about the results of her plan as she should have. She even felt a little disappointed.

Standing next to her at the refreshment stand was Randy Pratt, who had a particularly revolting way of mashing his cake and his ice cream into one large glob. Claire would have liked to walk away, but since he was the only other kid at the moment who was more interested in food than in valentines, she could hardly avoid him.

"So how many valentines did you get?" Randy asked, stuffing the glob into his face.

"Fourteen. How about you?"

"I got five," he said. "More than I expected, I guess."

"Five valentines isn't so bad," Claire said.

"But fourteen, that's fantastic," he said. "Not that I'm surprised you got so many."

"It's kind of nice," Claire said modestly. "It doesn't mean all that much, you know."

But while she was saying it, she was thinking how much more impressed she was by the number of valentines he had received. She looked over toward the other end of the cafeteria, where Shirley was pulling the last of the envelopes from the bin.

"One for Warren Fingler," Shirley yelled. "And here's another for Gaylord. And another for Gracie." Shirley handed out the cards. "The last one is for Claire."

Claire almost dropped her plate of ice cream and cake. Another valentine! Impossible! Did she make a mistake? Obviously she had counted wrong.

"Claire, aren't you going to get your valentine?" Randy asked.

"Oh, yeah. Sure," Claire said. She put her plate on the refreshment table and almost ran to Shirley. She took the envelope and looked at it as though it were another happy surprise. But this time her name on the envelope was not in her own handwriting.

Claire opened the envelope and pulled out the valentine. On the front was a drawing of a heart. She flipped the card open. On one side was a handwritten verse about roses and violets that she was in too much of a hurry to read. On the opposite side were the words "For Claire." Below that was the signature.

"Come on, Claire," Kimberly said. "Let us look at just one of your valentines."

"At least tell us who it's from," Gracie pleaded.

"Well, if you're really interested, take a look," Claire said. "By all means."

The musketeers grabbed the card.

"Oh, my," said Gracie.

"I've never . . ." gasped Margie.

"It's so romantic," exclaimed Kimberly.

"Who's it from?" Shirley asked.

"Is it okay to show it?" Gracie asked.

"Well, just that one," Claire said. "The others are too personal."

The musketeers handed the valentine to Shirley.

"Who sent it?" asked Warren Fingler. "Who's so romantic?"

"I don't know," Shirley said softly. "It's signed 'From your secret admirer.' "

A gasp went up from everyone standing around the love bin. Of all the valentines exchanged that day, only Claire's was from a secret admirer. As she looked at the faces around her, Claire knew she was the envy of all.

Especially Shirley.

Chapter Five

Her Secret Admirer

Claire was overwhelmed. If ever a girl had needed a secret admirer, she was it. She could only thank her lucky stars that hers had shown up in the nick of time. But it wasn't until she arrived home after school that she began to wonder just who her secret admirer could be. Maybe if she inspected the handwriting more closely, she might get a clue.

"Hi, Mom," Claire called, running up the stairs to her room. Without taking the time to remove either her coat or her scarf, she opened her briefcase and took out her valentines. She threw the fourteen she had written into the wastebasket. Then she placed the special valentine in the center of her desk and sat down and opened it very slowly.

The heart on the front was bright red. It looked like the heart on every other valentine, but Claire thought it was a lot prettier than the others. Then she read the verse that her secret admirer had written:

Roses are red
Violets are fine
Won't you please
Be my valentine?

Then Claire looked at the other side of the page. There it was, the best part:

For Claire,
From your secret admirer

Ever since she had learned to read and write, she hadn't paid much attention to anyone's handwriting. Still, she stared at the words, hoping that somehow they might give her a clue. The only sixth-grade handwriting she would have recognized was her own neat block letters. This handwriting was more like script, but not quite. The *o*'s were oddly shaped and the *t*'s were uncrossed.

The clock in the hall downstairs struck three thirty. She was late for her job, so Claire raced down the stairs, out the door, and along the slippery sidewalks to the video game parlor.

By the time she got there, she was almost out

of breath. She hung up her coat and apologized to Uncle Horace. It was the first time she had ever been late, and he didn't seem upset about it. Besides, it was one of those rare days when the money-changing machine was working and so were all the games. On those days, the video game parlor practically ran itself, though Claire would have been the last to admit it.

Valentine's Day or not, business was brisk. Warren Fingler was playing Moon Patrol, and Greg Stockard and Gaylord Adamson were playing Pac-Man together. The musketeers were, as usual, playing Ms. Pac-Man. Also as usual, Milton Marango was playing Donkey Kong. For once he was too engrossed in the game to do more than wave at Claire when she arrived.

Claire looked at the sixth-grade boys and wondered if one of them could be her secret admirer.

Gaylord was the best-looking boy at New Eden Middle, Claire thought. Although he seemed to pay an awful lot of attention to Shirley, it was still possible that he was Claire's secret admirer. And there was Greg Stockard. He wasn't quite as cute as Gaylord, but he was the best athlete in the school. Could he be the one? Maybe it was Arthur Lomax. Everyone in town said that Arthur was a musical genius. The thought that her secret admirer might be a genius was very appealing.

Claire turned toward Moon Patrol and wondered if Warren could be the one. He was good-looking *and* smart, but the year before she had beaten him out for the Junior Achievement Award. Claire decided he wasn't a very likely admirer. Not *hers,* anyway.

Claire tried to concentrate on her work, but she couldn't. By five thirty she realized that she had spent the whole afternoon trying to figure out who had sent that valentine. It was the sort of thing one would expect from Shirley Garfield. But not from Claire Van Kemp. She ought to be ashamed of herself.

Absentmindedly she emptied the quarters from the video games and added up the take for the day. Claire put all the quarters into small canvas sacks and carried them over to Uncle Horace. As she headed for the door, Claire heard a strange rumbling outside. A moment later the door opened and Shirley walked in, dragging the love bin behind her.

"I was afraid I'd be late," Shirley said. "I thought you might have closed up."

"Uncle Horace isn't in that much of a hurry for it," Claire said. "You could have returned it tomorrow. Or even the next day."

"I couldn't wait," Shirley said. "I wanted to tell you how sorry I am about our little argument the other day. Can you forgive me, Claire?"

"You know I'm always happy to accept an apology from you," Claire said.

"Thank you," Shirley said. "And congratulations on all your valentines. I was thrilled for you. By the way, is there any news about your secret admirer?"

"I've been trying to keep my mind on my job, Shirley," Claire said. "I don't have much time to go sleuthing."

"But, Claire," Shirley said. "It's the most exciting thing that ever happened. We're all guessing who could possibly have sent you that card."

"Well, maybe I'll never find out," Claire said, trying to conceal her own interest from Shirley. "Maybe I'd better leave well enough alone."

"I don't see why," Shirley said. "Somewhere out there a knight in shining armor is waiting for you."

"Well, he'll just have to keep waiting."

"Really, Claire, I don't see how you can let an opportunity like this go by."

"I've got a lot of other things to do with my time," Claire said. "Mature things like Van Kemperama."

"He could be dreamy," Shirley said teasingly.

"He could be a creep or a crank," Claire replied. "I could be opening a can of worms. Besides, I wouldn't have the slightest notion of how to find him, even if I wanted to, which I don't."

"The poor musketeers." Shirley sighed. "They'll be so disappointed."

"Well, thank them for their concern," Claire said. "But when it comes to some massive manhunt for my secret admirer, it's no dice."

"Do you promise me that you're not the slightest bit interested?" Shirley asked.

"Not the slightest bit," Claire said. "Finding out could be a big mistake. As you know, I'm not keen on making mistakes."

Shirley shrugged. "You can always change your mind," she said.

"If I do, you'll be the first to know," Claire said. She watched Shirley leave and prepared to follow. Claire was glad that Valentine's Day was over. As she walked home, she decided not to think about love bins or valentines or secret admirers anymore. Even though the day had been her personal triumph, Claire was still convinced that there was no future in valentines—or in secret admirers.

Chapter Six

The Most Likelies

Well, not completely.

If Claire had convinced herself *completely* that it didn't matter who her secret admirer was, she would have thrown the valentine away. But she didn't. That evening she tucked it away in a corner of the top drawer of her desk. She could take a look at her valentine every now and then, couldn't she?

The next day Claire let herself into the house, yelled, "Hi, Mom. I'm home," and ran upstairs to dump her books on her bed. When she came back down, her mother called from the kitchen, "Something arrived for you in the mail this morning."

"A package? A present from Grandma?" Claire asked.

"No, a letter. It's on the hall table."

Since everyone Claire knew lived in New

Eden, letters were rare. Just about the only ones she ever received were invitations to birthday parties.

Claire opened the envelope and took out a single sheet of white paper. She unfolded it. It read, "*I cherish you. Your secret admirer.*" Claire ran upstairs and put it in her desk drawer. Then she went to work.

The next day there was another note. It read, "*I worship the ground you walk on.*"

The day after, another note was waiting. Same paper. Same handwriting. This time the note read, "*I adore you.*"

That evening Claire pulled the three notes and the valentine from her drawer and lined them up on her desk. Who on earth could her admirer be? Even though Claire told herself that it didn't matter, the question was beginning to eat away at her.

She pulled out a piece of paper and wrote down the names of all the boys in her class. Then Claire had an idea. She would write down all her best qualities, examine the list of boys, and decide which boy would be most likely to admire her.

First Claire wrote INTELLIGENT. She crossed that out and wrote EXTREMELY INTELLIGENT. Not all boys were attracted to intelligent girls,

Claire knew, so maybe her extreme intelligence would rule out some of her classmates.

HARD-WORKING was what Claire wrote down next. That ought to eliminate the lazy boys. Claire stuck the end of her pen into her mouth and tried to think up some more of her most admirable qualities.

Underneath HARD-WORKING she wrote BEAUTIFUL, but she crossed that out right away and replaced it with ATTRACTIVE.

She looked at her list:

~~INTELLIGENT~~ EXTREMELY INTELLIGENT
HARD-WORKING
~~BEAUTIFUL~~ ATTRACTIVE

If Claire wrote down *all* her admirable qualities, it would take her all night. Three were enough for now. With several flourishes, she crossed off the names of the boys who were not extremely intelligent, hard-working, or attractive. Then she came to Warren's name. He was all three, but there was no way he would have sent the notes. Ever since she had beat him out for the last Junior Achievement Award, they had hardly spoken. She crossed his name off the list.

Three names were left: Gaylord, Arthur, and Greg.

The next day, as soon as the bell rang for lunch, Claire jumped to her feet. Because she sat in the last row, she was usually the last out of the classroom. Today, however, she wasn't about to let Arthur Lomax get too far ahead of her.

"Arthur?" she asked at the cafeteria door, panting a little from having run so fast.

"Claire?" Arthur asked. "Is something wrong? You seem out of breath."

"Don't worry about me," Claire gasped. "I just wanted to ask you a question."

"Okay," Arthur said. "Shoot."

"Is life lonely for you, Arthur?"

"Huh?"

"I mean your being a musical genius," Claire explained. "Doesn't it get lonely for you, practicing at the piano all by yourself every afternoon? Don't you ever yearn for a special friend?"

"Just because I'm a musical prodigy doesn't mean I don't have friends," Arthur said a little defensively.

"I said a *special* friend," Claire said. "Wouldn't you like to have a special friend? Do you know what I mean, Arthur?"

Now Arthur looked more bewildered than defensive. "I guess I don't know what you mean, Claire," he said, shaking his head. "I think all my friends are special."

Then he walked quickly to the end of the lunch line.

Since Claire had to keep things subtle, she decided it would be impossible to approach either Greg or Gaylord while they were eating. At New Eden Middle boys ate with boys and girls ate with girls. So Claire sat down with Marcie Lewis and wolfed down her egg-salad sandwich. When she noticed Greg getting up from his table, Claire followed him out of the cafeteria.

She found him standing by the water fountain.

"Greg," she said as he stepped back and wiped his mouth. "Did I ever tell you how much I admire you?"

"I don't think so," Greg said. "Why should you?"

"Because you're the best athlete in the school," Claire said. "I'm not much of an athlete myself, but I do admire athletes a lot, and I wanted you to know."

"Thanks, Claire," Greg said. "It's nice of you to say so." Greg turned around and started to walk away. With two steps Claire caught up with him again.

"I think it's too bad I didn't tell you before," Claire said.

"Don't worry about it," Greg said.

"But I do," Claire replied. "I just can't help thinking it's too bad when you admire someone but you don't tell them. You can understand that, can't you?"

"I guess so," he said.

"I mean, someone might be too shy to tell someone else they admire them," Claire said. "It's perfectly understandable."

"I didn't know you were shy, Claire."

"I'm not shy," she said. "But I could understand it if you were."

"Gee, I don't think so," Greg said. "When I admire someone, I tell them."

"Always, Greg?" Claire asked.

"Why not?"

Greg walked away, and Claire didn't even try to catch up with him.

Claire's last but most likely candidate was Gaylord Adamson. There were two reasons why he was at the top of her list. The first was that he was the best-looking boy in the school. The second was that he and Shirley Garfield hung out together. Not that they dated or anything, because in New Eden twelve is too young for that. But they did go to parties together, and they walked home almost every afternoon together. Because of Shirley, it made perfect sense to Claire that Gaylord would want to keep his admiration for her a secret.

As Claire was leaving school that day, she saw Gaylord standing at the main entrance to the building. He was holding two stacks of textbooks. The second stack must have been Shirley's,

Claire decided. Gaylord was probably waiting to walk her home, as usual.

"Gaylord," Claire said, walking up to him. "Your family has traveled all over the world, and that's why I thought you might be able to answer a question for me."

"You want travel tips?" Gaylord asked.

"Oh, no," Claire said. "I'm not planning a trip at the moment. What I wanted to ask you was of a slightly different nature. Something you might know from seeing how people live in a lot of different countries."

"I don't think I know anything like that," Gaylord said.

"Please try," Claire said. "It's very important to me. What I was wondering about was if people are able to admire more than one person at a time. From your own observation, do you think that's possible?"

"Well, I can only speak for myself," Gaylord said.

"That's the only person I want you to speak for," Claire said softly.

"Well, I admire lots of people."

"At the same time?"

"Sure," Gaylord said. "There's nothing wrong with that, is there?"

"It might be a little awkward," Claire said. "It might even make for bad feelings."

"I don't see why," Gaylord said. "I admire

the President of the United States and the astronauts and all sorts of sports stars. I don't see why any of them would get upset about my admiring them all at the same time."

From the corner of her eye Claire could see Shirley walking down the hall. She didn't seem very happy to see Claire talking to Gaylord.

"Well, I've got to run," Claire said. "I can't tell you how interesting your comments are to me, Gaylord."

"Sure, Claire," Gaylord said.

"See you around," Claire said.

She opened the main door and left the school. As she got on the bus, she tried to add up the pluses and minuses of her search. The balance, she realized, was the same as it had been before. On the one hand, she still hadn't found her secret admirer. But on the other hand, she still couldn't rule out her three major candidates.

Chapter Seven

Better Luck Next Time

Even though Claire had to admit to herself that her questions might have been too subtle, she decided that the question-and-answer plan of attack was never going to work. What she needed was a way to outsmart her secret admirer without him even suspecting.

That afternoon was a busy one at Van Kemperama. Sometimes when Claire had a problem she couldn't solve, she liked to keep busy. But the secret admirer problem demanded immediate attention. Besides, Claire couldn't ignore the very strong feeling that her secret admirer was only a few steps away from her. So, that afternoon while Claire tried to act like her old self, she really didn't feel like her old self.

Every day Claire stayed on to empty the machines of their quarters and prepare them for Uncle Horace. But one night a week Claire stayed later than usual to take the quarters that were going back into the money-changing machine to the back room of the store and dump them into the sink there. Then she would pour two capfuls of Woolite over them and fill the sink with lukewarm water. After five minutes she would take out the quarters one by one, rinse them off, and dry them with paper towels.

It had been Claire's own idea to wash the quarters once a week. From what she had read in the newspapers recently, she knew it wouldn't be long before some of the parents in New Eden began to worry that their children were spending too much money and too much time at Van Kemperama. It had happened in other towns, and there was no reason to believe that it couldn't happen in New Eden too.

That was why Claire washed the quarters. It was good public relations, she thought. She had even put up a sign by the money-changing machine that read:

VAN KEMPERAMA
IS PLEASED TO ANNOUNCE
THAT ALL THE QUARTERS IN OUR GAMES AND MACHINES
ARE WASHED WEEKLY IN FULL ACCORDANCE
WITH THE NEW EDEN BOARD OF HEALTH AND SANITATION
STANDARDS.
SINCERELY YOURS,
THE MANAGEMENT

As Claire watched the bubbles cover the quarters and began to swirl them around with her hands, she thought about her secret admirer. He might be clever, but Claire couldn't believe that he was going to outsmart her for long.

What Claire needed was a brilliant new plan, and she needed it right away. She perched on her stool and stared into the sink, as if the soapsuds would provide the answer. They didn't. Claire let the water out of the sink and reached for the roll of paper towels on the wall. Slowly and methodically she rinsed the quarters and dried them off. If they were in the least bit wet when she returned them to the money-changing machine, rust would set in and the machine would be out of order permanently.

"If only I had a crystal ball," she said to herself as she stacked the quarters in neat piles. Though Claire didn't believe in magic, she knew that some people did. They believed in crystal balls and palm reading and astrology. Once she had seen an advertisement from a woman who could tell what your future would be just by examining your handwriting.

Suddenly a little tingle went through her body, just as it always did when she was on the verge of one of her major ideas. Claire would find that ad and send the valentine and the three notes to that woman.

It was as simple as that. A moment later,

however, Claire realized it wasn't. What if it were all a fraud and the handwriting expert wasn't an expert after all? Besides, Claire wasn't sure where she had seen the ad. Handwriting experts weren't the sort of people you looked up in the New Eden Yellow Pages.

For once Claire thought that the trouble with New Eden was that it was too small. Every other town in the country must have at least one reputable handwriting expert around. Then again, once New Eden had been the only town in the world without a video game parlor. But thanks to none other than Claire Van Kemp, that had been taken care of. If only there were some other overachiever who would set up a handwriting business.

That was the magic moment when Claire's little tingle turned into a major *ting.* Thrilled once more by her own cleverness, Claire turned out the lights and locked up the store. By the time she got home that night, the plan was perfected.

The next afternoon Claire approached Uncle Horace.

"You know, Uncle Horace," Claire said, "I've finally figured out what's wrong with Van Kemperama."

"What can be wrong?" Uncle Horace asked. "Thanks to you, business is booming."

"Right now it is," Claire said. "But that

doesn't mean it will always boom. From what I've seen, you've got to keep bringing in new stuff. Otherwise the customers get bored."

"If you're talking about Milton Marango, forget it," Uncle Horace said. "I talked to the video game distributor again last week, and there's nothing more sophisticated than what we've got right now. If you want me to speak to Milton, I will."

"Oh, no," Claire said. "I wasn't thinking about Milton. He hasn't complained in days. I was thinking of a different kind of gimmick to attract people."

"You were?"

"I was thinking of a special event."

"Such as?" Uncle Horace asked nervously.

"Maybe a handwriting analyst," Claire said. "That's just a possibility, of course."

"Of course," Uncle Horace said. "How on earth did you ever think up that one?"

"I've been noticing how interested most of the kids are in having their handwriting analyzed."

"You want me to hire someone full-time just to analyze kids' handwriting?" Uncle Horace asked.

"I thought we could do it on a trial basis," Claire explained. "I'd just put up a curtain in Van Kemperama and see if anyone comes. If no one does, I'll just take down the curtain."

"And where are we supposed to find a handwriting expert?" Uncle Horace asked.

"That's where you're in luck," Claire said. "It just so happens that handwriting analysis is one of my specialties."

"I'm not surprised," Uncle Horace said. "I've got to admit it, Claire. You never cease to amaze."

"Then it's okay?"

"If you're willing to do all the work," Uncle Horace said, "I'm willing to let you do it. I just don't want you to be hurt if the handwriting business doesn't work out very well."

"Thanks, Uncle Horace," Claire said. "But I'm not afraid to take risks. Nothing ventured, nothing gained, I always say."

But as Claire walked back to the video game parlor, she knew there was no risk whatsoever. Even if her newest business venture lasted only one afternoon, that was long enough to find out once and for all who her secret admirer was.

Chapter Eight

Madame Claire Voyante

The next day Claire tacked posters on all the bulletin boards at school, announcing that Van Kemperama was proud to present the world-famous handwriting analyst, Madame Claire Voyante, for a limited engagement. She also handed out little leaflets to anyone who might have missed the posters. In the afternoon Claire stayed late at the store to set up the handwriting analysis booth.

Since Van Kemp's did not stock window curtains, Claire used a dark-blue plastic shower curtain instead. Behind it she put two chairs and a table. Then she tacked up two of her posters on the shower curtain and left a pile of her leaflets next to the money-changing machine.

What was a handwriting expert supposed to look like? Claire wondered. What should she wear?

On her way home Claire stopped at the New Eden Five and Ten and bought a black fright wig. *That* seemed right. After all, handwriting experts were supposed to look mysterious, even a little bit like witches. Then she bought two dollars worth of junk jewelry to put around her neck and wrists. Handwriting experts probably looked like overdressed witches.

At dinner that night Claire was so absorbed in trying to figure out the rest of Madame Claire Voyante's costume that she hardly listened to what her parents were saying.

"Mom?" Claire asked, without realizing that she was interrupting. "May I borrow your kimono next week?"

"The black one with the little cabbage roses all over it?" her mother asked.

"That's the one," Claire said.

"What do you need it for?" her mother asked. "Have you been invited to a costume party?"

"It's for my handwriting analysis business," Claire explained. "I need to wear something really special for it."

"It's a little long for you, Claire," her mother said.

"I'll pin it up," she said. "I'll make sure it doesn't get ripped or dirty."

"All right," her mother said. "You can use it

this time. After that, you'll have to get yourself another costume."

"One day is all I'll need it for," Claire said.

Claire was pleased. Everything had been taken care of. With planning like that, how could she fail?

Four days later Madame Claire Voyante made her debut. All dressed up in her wig, her jewelry, and her mother's kimono, Claire peeked out from behind the shower curtain.

Everyone from New Eden Middle was at Van Kemperama, it seemed. With a flourish she pushed the curtain aside and stepped forward.

"Madame Claire Voyante is open for business," Claire announced loudly. "Please form a line to the left. Madame Claire will analyze each of you individually."

"You're Madame Claire Voyante?" Shirley asked.

"The one and only," Claire replied.

"I was expecting someone a little older, I guess," Shirley said. "How much is this handwriting analysis going to cost?"

"How much?" Claire repeated. She realized that she hadn't planned her new business venture down to the last detail. She looked at Shirley and the others in line. Then she looked around the video game parlor and saw to her horror that some of the boys, including her prime candidates, were not in line. It was time to think fast. "As a special introductory offer, Madame Claire Voyante will analyze handwriting free of charge to Van Kemperama's regular clientele."

The boys looked up from their games. Arthur even started to make his way toward the end of the line.

"Where did you get those clothes, Claire?" Shirley asked.

"It's regulation handwriting analyst gear," Claire said as she ushered Shirley into the booth and closed the curtain behind her. "And while I'm on duty, it's Madame Claire. Sit down and show me some handwriting."

"I have my English theme from last week," Shirley said as she took a piece of paper from her purse and handed it to Claire.

"You got a B plus on it," Claire said.

"I don't need a handwriting analyst to tell me that," Shirley said.

"Let me study it a little more closely," Claire said. She held the paper up to her eyes and pretended to be studying it. Then she passed it back to Shirley. "Your handwriting reveals what everyone in town has known about you all along, Shirley."

"What's that supposed to mean?" Shirley asked, looking a little bit frightened.

"Nothing to worry about, my dear," Claire said reassuringly. This was no time to offend her first customer, even if she was Shirley Garfield. "Your handwriting shows that you are as lovely on the inside as you are on the outside."

Shirley relaxed a little. "What about my future?"

"Everything you always wanted it to be," Claire said. "You must be overjoyed."

"I was hoping you could be a little more specific," Shirley said.

"For free, Madame Claire doesn't get specific," Claire said. "Come back another time, dear. The price will be only twenty-five cents."

If Shirley didn't look exactly thrilled, she did look at least pacified. She stood up and walked back to the video games.

"Next!" Madame Claire shouted.

Gracie Arnold stepped inside.

In two minutes Claire told Gracie that her shyness was her most likable quality. Then she explained to Marcie Lewis that she would be the most beautiful girl in New Eden once her braces were removed. After that she told Kimberly Horowitz that she was far more popular than she had ever imagined. Since she couldn't think of anything new to tell Margie Neustadt, she told her the same thing.

Claire told Randy Pratt that he had a very good sense of humor. She told Vincent Jefferson that he was smart. Then she told Hal Rilling that his handwriting was very nice but that he should work on his spelling.

Madame Claire's customers were so satisfied that Claire was beginning to feel that she really did know something about analyzing handwriting. If things kept up, maybe Madame Claire's first appearance would not be her last. When she dismissed her next customer and saw Arthur and Greg and Gaylord standing next in line, however, she remembered the main purpose of the day's event.

"Welcome, Arthur," she said. "Please sit down. Is there anything in particular you want to know?"

Arthur handed Claire a piece of paper. It was a history exam they had taken the week before. "I'd like to know if I'm really going to be famous."

Claire looked at the exam. "You're going to be famous, Arthur. Don't worry about it."

"How famous?"

"Write a little more down on this pad," Claire commanded, "and Madame Claire will tell you."

"Like what?"

"Try 'Roses are red' for starters," Claire suggested. When Arthur had written the words, Claire took a look. "World-famous, the way I see it."

As Arthur got up to leave, Claire tore off the

top sheet and stuffed the piece of paper into the pocket of her kimono. Then she let Greg Stockard take his turn.

"Write down 'love and adore,' " Claire said as soon as Greg took his seat. When he passed the pad back to her, she took out her magnifying glass and examined the words. "You haven't yet selected your path of greatness, Greg," Claire said. "It will come to you as a surprise. Maybe in sports. Maybe not. But it's there."

The next in line was Gaylord. As soon as he sat down, he handed Claire a note with his handwriting on it.

Claire took a look. "I need a little more to go on," she said. "Would you write 'the ground you walk on'? That might do the trick."

Gaylord wrote the words on the pad.

"You are a man who knows his own heart," Claire said. "You also know the value of a dollar."

Claire waited until Gaylord stood up.

"Nice doing business with you, Gaylord," she said as she watched him leave the booth. She opened the curtain to see if anyone was left.

"My turn?" Warren Fingler asked as he took a step toward Madame Claire's booth.

"Gee, Warren," Claire said. "Do you really want your handwriting analyzed? It's getting pretty late in the afternoon."

"I know," Warren said. "I've been waiting in line for almost two hours."

"I'm afraid that Madame Claire's head is a little blurry," Claire said. "She's not used to so much turnover."

Warren frowned. Then his frown turned into a scowl. Claire decided that she had no choice but to welcome him into Madame Claire's den. Her examination of Gaylord's and Greg's and Arthur's handwriting would have to wait.

"Well, I'll give it my best shot," Claire announced. "Don't be disappointed if I don't live up to my reputation."

Warren sat down. "What would you like me to write down?" he asked.

"Anything that comes to mind," Claire said.

Warren picked up a pen and started to write, then handed the pad to Claire.

"Roses are red," Claire read. Although she wasn't absolutely certain that she had ever seen the handwriting before, a terrific *ting* went through her body.

"Is there anything you can tell me about what my life is going to be like?" Warren asked.

"Tell me why you wrote those words," Claire said anxiously.

"I saw them on one of the Valentine's Day cards in my mother's store," Warren answered. "I guess they just stuck."

Did he really expect her to believe *that?* Claire wondered. Claire wanted to blurt out that she knew he was her secret admirer. Who else

would have written those words? She caught her breath and thought again. Warren must have a special reason for being secretive. She would have to follow his lead. "Yes, Warren," she said, her voice trembling a little. "There's a lot I can tell you. I just don't know where to begin."

"Begin at the beginning," Warren suggested.

"I must ask you some questions first," she said. "Do you ever feel shy, Warren? Are you ever timid about coming right out and saying what you think?"

"I guess I am," he said thoughtfully. "That's true enough."

"And is it even harder for you to express what you feel?"

"Sometimes," Warren admitted.

"Does the word 'everlasting' mean anything special to you?" Claire asked.

"It means forever," Warren said. "I'd say that forever is something special. Now can you tell me what my future is going to be like?"

"If you can be a little less timid about expressing yourself, your future could be very beautiful."

"That's it?" Warren asked. "Can't you say more?"

"Not here," Claire said. "Not now. We should talk someplace where it's quieter, someplace where we'll have more privacy."

"Then you'll tell me what's going to happen?" Warren asked. "Can I call you tomorrow?"

"That would be perfect," Claire said. She looked into his eyes. Had they always been so brown? she wondered.

"Thanks, Claire," Warren said. "I'm really looking forward to talking some more with you."

"So am I," Claire said as she watched him disappear beyond the curtain.

All along it had been Warren, and Claire had never even suspected. How wrong she had been to cross him off her list. Claire tossed the other boys' handwriting samples in the wastebasket. She sat back in her chair and closed her eyes. The day had been exhausting, but it certainly had been profitable, even though she hadn't made a dime. Her plan had turned out to be every bit as brilliant as she had hoped it would be.

She stood up and walked from Madame Claire's booth into the video game parlor. It was late in the afternoon and the place was empty—except for Milton Marango, of course, who was still playing away at the Donkey Kong game.

"It's time to call it a day, Milton," she said.

"So soon?" Milton asked.

"Okay, Milton," she said patiently. "I'll analyze your handwriting, but after that you'll have to go."

"I'll go now," Milton said. He picked up his books and his coat.

"Don't you want me to examine your handwriting?" Claire asked.

"No, thanks, Claire," Milton said. "I'm probably late for dinner. How did your business go?"

"Better than I ever expected," Claire said.

"I'm glad for you," Milton said.

As Milton left Van Kemperama, Claire's thoughts returned to Warren. How very nice it was to have someone like him for her secret admirer, someone so good-looking and someone who was bright, too, she thought.

Claire wondered if maybe Shirley Garfield did know what she was talking about after all.

Chapter Nine

Her Wildest Dreams

As long as Warren wanted to keep his secret admirer status a secret, Claire had to go along with it. For the time being, she would have to suppress the urge to tell Shirley or the musketeers. If Warren learned that his cover was blown, he would probably become more timid than he already was. Worse still, he might even be mad at her.

As Claire had learned from her plan to discover the identity of her secret admirer, the key to any major foolproof scheme was subtlety and patience. From now on she was going to exercise both those qualities. Naturally, she would be a lot nicer to Warren than she had been in the past. If circumstances demanded it, Claire would be downright charming. Not that she thought that would be hard to pull off. So what if she didn't know how to bat her eyes and giggle the way

Shirley did? Once you knew someone already liked you, being nice to him was as easy as pie.

Someday Warren would tell her the whole story. They would be walking along Main Street on their way to the Hot Shoppe, laughing at some private joke. Claire would say something like "Gee, Warren, I always have such a good time with you," and Warren would say something like "Same here, Claire." She would tell him how funny and bright he was, and he would act surprised. Then he would say something like "You know, Claire, I've always admired you."

Then it would be Claire's turn to pretend to be surprised. She would say something like "I don't believe you, Warren," and he would say, "Oh, but it's true." She would shake her head and laugh a little, and he would say, "Oh, Claire, don't you know?" "Know what?" she would ask. Then he would say, "That I'm your secret admirer. Don't you know that I'm the one who sent you the valentine and all those notes?"

Claire would open her briefcase and pull out the notes and the valentine, which she carried with her always. Warren would hand her his homework assignment to prove that the handwriting matched.

They would laugh again and go off to the Hot Shoppe for a milk shake to celebrate. The shakes would be the thick kind with an extra scoop of ice cream, but neither of them would mind paying extra. In fact, they would insist on treating each other.

From then on, their afternoon breaks at the Hot Shoppe before Van Kemperama opened would become a well-known ritual. On school nights they might study together at the library, and on weekends they might go to an early movie or see a basketball game at the high school.

Just as Claire and Warren were walking home from the game, the alarm clock rang. Claire rolled over in her bed and shut it off. The movies, the basketball game, and the milk shakes had been a dream. For a moment Claire wondered what was happening. Until very recently her dreams had been about video games and Junior Achievement Awards.

She got out of bed and walked to the bathroom to brush her teeth. Looking closely at herself in the mirror, she wondered if she were becoming boy-crazy. Although Claire wasn't exactly sure, she didn't think she looked as if she were. It was just that these new dreams were making her feel odd.

Claire wondered why Warren hadn't called her yet. Two days before, he had wanted to see her right away about discussing his future. He had promised to call her, but he hadn't. Claire wondered if she had been stood up. But no one could stand up someone he loved, worshiped, and admired. As Claire got dressed and went downstairs to breakfast, she decided that Warren just had a case of cold feet.

That had to be it. For the last forty-eight hours Warren had probably spent his afternoons and evenings nervously sitting by the telephone, trying to summon up the courage to call her. When she had seen him at school the day before, he had waved to her but he hadn't said anything. Although Claire thought it absolutely imperative to maintain her subtle attitude, she was losing patience. If she were too patient for too long, she had a feeling that she and Warren would never get to have that milk shake at the Hot Shoppe.

Claire gulped down her orange juice, wolfed down her cereal, put on her coat and mittens, and raced out of the house before her parents could point out that the school bus wasn't due for another fifteen minutes. Today, however, Claire wouldn't be taking the bus. Warren's house was seven blocks from hers. If she hurried, she would be there before he left for school.

When she got to the Finglers' block, Claire stopped short. She had made it in record time, and her huffing and puffing proved it. She took ten deep breaths and began to walk along the sidewalk. Just as Warren's house came into view, the front door opened and Warren walked out.

"What are you doing here?" Warren asked as soon as he saw her. "How come you're not waiting for the bus at your house?"

"I'm not riding the bus this morning," Claire said. "I'm taking my morning constitutional. What a pretty house you live in, Warren. I guess I forgot you lived on this block."

"I've lived on this block all my life," he said.

"Of course, you have," Claire said agreeably. "My mistake. Everyone forgets things now and then, don't they?"

"I guess so," Warren said.

"Like our meeting, for instance," she said. "We were going to talk about the future, Warren."

"I've been awfully busy with the present," Warren said. "I really didn't forget."

"Well, you know what I always say," Claire said.

"What do you always say?" he asked.

"I always say that when it comes to the future, there's no time like the present. Are you ready, Warren?"

"Ready for what?" Warren asked cautiously.

"For the future," Claire replied. She took a few steps along the sidewalk. Warren fell in with her. She hoped he wouldn't ask if he could carry her briefcase. As pleased as she was to have him for her secret admirer, she still had her standards.

"Do you have more information about my future?" Warren asked.

"Your handwriting says you have everything it takes," Claire said. "The world will be your oyster if you play your cards right, Warren."

"You see that much?"

"Take my word for it," Claire said.

"Since when did you get to know so much about handwriting?" Warren asked. "Did you take a course or something?"

"No, nothing like that," Claire said. "It's more like a gift. You have it or you don't. Of course, I respond to some people's handwriting more than I do to others'. I can't be sure all the time."

"But you're sure about mine?"

"I respond to your handwriting, Warren," Claire said. "I hope that doesn't embarrass you."

"If everything's going to be okay, I can take it," Warren said.

"You have nothing to worry about," Claire said, hoping to build up his self-confidence. "Especially in the field of interpersonal relationships."

"That means friends?"

"That's a very sensitive way of putting it," Claire said.

Claire thought that a bright spot on the interpersonal relationship horizon would be to ask

Warren if he would take her to the presentation of the Jaycee's Junior Achievement Award. But maybe she should wait until it was official. Besides, she didn't want to remind Warren of last year, when she had won and he had lost. That sort of thing could undermine anyone's self-confidence.

Before Claire could come up with a plan, she and Warren were passing Shirley Garfield's house.

"Hey, guys, wait for me," Shirley called to them. For all the world Claire wished that Shirley hadn't seen her with Warren. She prayed that it would never occur to Shirley that something was up in the secret admirer department.

"Hi, Shirley," Warren said.

"Hi," Claire said.

"Since when did you start walking to school?" Shirley asked.

"Since Claire took up her morning constitutional," Warren explained.

"Since when was that?"

"Since this morning," Claire said.

"Both of you?" Shirley asked. "Constitutionals? Together?"

"Yeah," Warren said. "Claire just happened to be walking by my house, so I joined her."

"What a lovely coincidence," Shirley said. "If it's a coincidence. I hope I'm not interrupting anything."

"Not at all," Warren said.

"Are you sure, Claire?"

"Yes, Shirley," Claire said. "Sure, I'm sure."

Claire looked straight ahead and hoped that Shirley wasn't looking at her. For the first time in her life, Claire Van Kemp was blushing.

Chapter Ten

A Change in the Climate

In New Eden winter does not turn into spring with one magical flourish. In between the two seasons is a period that the people of New Eden call mud-time. The sun gets warm enough to turn the snow on the ground and the ice on the ponds back into water. By the beginning of April the air is warmer and sweeter. The grass brightens up considerably, and buds can be spotted on trees and bushes.

As Claire would have been the first to tell you, the video game business makes no allowances for seasons. Rain or shine, warm or cold, kids play video games. Oh, sure, there was a little drop-off in business when baseball practice began, and Claire noticed that Saturday afternoons weren't quite so frantic anymore. But no matter what, there was still change to be made, quarters to be washed, and customers to be catered to.

One customer in particular. In the last few weeks Warren had been dropping by almost every day. Sometimes he played at the games awhile, and sometimes he just spent time talking with Claire. Claire enjoyed those moments the best, especially if Shirley wasn't around. The other kids were customers, but Warren was more like a friend. When they were talking about school or the other kids, Claire found herself forgetting all about work. Sometimes she even forgot about the Junior Achievement Award.

But only for a moment. If you were going to make something of yourself, you had to make a few sacrifices along the way. If you wanted to win a Junior Achievement Award two years in a row, you couldn't complain about not having as much time as you wanted for yourself or your friends. Claire had her list of priorities to keep in mind. Van Kemperama and the Junior Achievement Award were still at the top.

Claire wasn't sure where Warren fit on that list. Though it was more fun to be with him during the afternoons than it was to run the business, something about Warren had begun to bother her. It had been almost a month since their first morning constitutional, and still he hadn't spoken up. Claire was beginning to wonder how *anyone* could be that timid. She even wondered if her secret admirer was having second thoughts.

"Any luck with the S.A.?" Shirley asked one day after gym.

"What essay?" Claire asked. "We don't have an assignment this week."

"Not that kind of essay." Shirley giggled. "S.A. as in secret admirer. Have you made any progress?"

"I haven't thought about my secret admirer in months," Claire said. "He's probably moved to another town."

"Not even a clue?"

"Not even a clue."

"You're not holding out on us, are you, Claire?" Shirley asked. "You know the musketeers and I can keep a secret."

"I'll remember that," Claire said, although she didn't see how any of the girls in her class could keep a secret as thrilling as hers.

Finally Shirley gave up. Still, it seemed to Claire that she was having the same conversation almost every day with someone else. It was beginning to make her nervous. Better to think about business and the prospect of winning her Junior Achievement Award.

As the middle of April rolled around, Claire could see that she had the overachievement field to herself. The musketeers, it was true, had sold an unusually large amount of Girl Scout Cookies in March. Arthur Lomax had given a piano recital at the church, but only twenty people came. And Gaylord had won an honorable mention for a short story he had submitted to a magazine. Admirable as those achievements were, they simply were not on a par with what Claire had done with Van Kemperama. Besides, the Junior Chamber of Commerce in New Eden was very big on rewarding those who made money. Writing short stories and giving recitals and selling Girl Scout Cookies couldn't compare with the results she was getting.

In fact, Claire was so sure of victory that she surprised even herself about how calm she was when Principal Pringle's voice came over the loudspeaker that fateful day.

"Good morning, boys and girls," Mr. Pringle said. "It is my pleasure to announce this year's winner of the Junior Chamber of Commerce's Junior Achievement Award. As I'm sure all of you know, the award goes to a youngster in New Eden who in the last year has on his or her own initiative made a recognizable achievement in the field of business, the arts, or public service."

As Mr. Pringle paused to take a breath, so did Claire. She folded her hands and sat up straighter. Several people turned around to get a glimpse of her. Warren turned around, too, and gave her the V-for-victory sign. Claire's modest little smile turned into a beam, which she quickly corrected. It wasn't a good thing to look too sure of yourself. Claire would have to do her best to look surprised, although she knew she had to be careful. If she overdid the surprise routine, no one would fall for that, either. From past experience she knew that winning awards had to be handled very carefully.

"This year," Mr. Pringle went on, "I am happy to report that more students than ever have outdone themselves in all the areas I mentioned. On behalf of all the faculty at the school, I want to offer our congratulations to the many boys and girls who have made outstanding contributions to our town."

Several more heads turned around to look in Claire's direction. She didn't look at any of them, but she kept the little smile on her face. Even though winning them was the best thing about awards, Claire hoped that all the losers would find comfort in Mr. Pringle's words.

"Of course, there can be only one winner," Mr. Pringle was saying. "This year's award committee has had a tough time coming to a decision. However, after much discussion, there was one individual whose initiative and imagination were especially outstanding. That is why I am sure you will all join me in congratulating this year's Junior Achievement Award winner, Milton Marango."

Milton Marango? From the way her classmates were shaking their heads, Claire knew they were as surprised as she was. But none of them could possibly be as horrified.

"Over the past few months, Milton Marango has spent his afternoons and evenings inventing a new video game," Mr. Pringle said. "A month ago, Milton sent his game to Utubi, a video game company in Tokyo, and last week the Junior Chamber of Commerce received word that Utubi has bought Milton's game and will be distributing it throughout the United States and Japan. In addition to the satisfaction that Milton must feel from having sold his game, Milton has also received a check for a quarter of a million yen as an advance against future earnings. His parents are putting the money toward his college education.

"Although the formal ceremony won't take place for several more weeks, I am sure all the students here will be eager to congratulate Milton Marango on his splendid achievement. Thank you."

Mrs. Simkins started to write some dates on the blackboard. Everyone picked up a pencil and started taking notes. Claire picked up hers, but she didn't write down anything, because she couldn't concentrate. All she could hear were the words "Milton Marango" repeating themselves over and over again in her brain. "Milton Marango. Winner of the Junior Achievement Award."

For the life of her Claire couldn't tell at that moment whether she was more shocked that she had lost the award or that Milton Marango had won it.

Chapter Eleven

Green-eyed Monsters

That afternoon Claire did something she had never done since Van Kemperama had opened. When she got home from school, she called Uncle Horace and told him that she couldn't work that day. When he asked if she were sick, she said yes, and promised that she would be in the next day.

She didn't mean to mislead Uncle Horace, but in her heart she felt that it was very unlikely that she would ever feel better. It had taken all her strength just to stumble through the rest of the day at school. She had barely been able to eat half her bologna sandwich. Claire knew that the only reason she ate at all was to avoid the awful silence that arose when she sat down with Shirley and Gracie. Both of them must have known how upset she was about the award, but since they knew there were no words that could console her, they didn't try to say anything.

Still, Shirley and Gracie had tried to smile. And Warren had waved to her from the table where he was sitting with some other boys. The most that Claire could hope for was that the little trace of a smile was still plastered to her face.

When Claire put down the phone after talking to Uncle Horace, she felt some of the shock wearing off, but she couldn't begin to get over her disbelief. She had read about little kids who did brilliant things, but it would take forever to accept the fact that little Milton Marango was one of them. To think that Milton had won *her* award made her angry all over again.

Claire walked up the stairs and dropped her briefcase on her bed. Ordinarily, she figured out how long it would take her to do her homework assignments so she knew how much time she would have left over for television. Today it didn't matter. As far as Claire was concerned, nothing mattered anymore.

In the past when she had been disappointed about things, she talked it over with her mother or her father and soon she would start to feel okay again. But this afternoon, even if one of her parents had been home, she wouldn't have said a word about losing the award. If someone tried to cheer her up, it would only make her feel worse. Losing what she had worked so hard and so long for wasn't something she would get over in a couple of hours.

Still, Claire knew that she didn't want to be alone right now. She went to the kitchen and poured herself a glass of milk. Two gulps later she was looking up the Finglers' number in the telephone book. She dialed. After four rings Warren answered.

Without saying a word, Claire hung up. He wouldn't want to listen to her problems. Even if he did, she couldn't bear telling them to him. She didn't want anyone in New Eden, Warren especially, to think she was feeling sorry for herself.

There was a knock at the kitchen door. Uncle Horace walked in.

"Hi, Claire," he said. "Mr. Grey is taking care of the store for a bit. You're feeling better, I hope."

"Maybe a little," she said, hoping that she hadn't given Uncle Horace the impression that she was very sick. "How are things at Van Kemperama?"

"Terrific," Uncle Horace said. "Milton Marango is there signing autographs. He asked after you, Claire."

Claire shuddered. "I guess you heard about the Junior Achievement Award."

"Everyone's talking about it," Uncle Horace said. "I wondered if maybe that was what had you down."

"I don't want anyone to think I'm a poor loser, so I'm not going to admit it, even if it's true."

"I think you're allowed," he said, putting his hand on her shoulder.

"Well, I hope you didn't come here to feel sorry for me," Claire said. "I feel sorry enough for me without any outside help."

"I have some news I thought might cheer you up a little," Uncle Horace said. "If you don't think you can stand it, we can talk another time."

"You could give it a try."

"Milton says you deserve a lot of the credit for his video game," Uncle Horace said. "He says you gave him the idea for it in the first place."

Claire sat down at the kitchen table. With a bitter pang she remembered that afternoon. She hadn't meant to encourage him, only to get rid of him for a while. "I'm responsible for his winning?" she asked.

"I'm afraid you're going to have to take some of the credit for it," Uncle Horace said. "I thought that might make you feel a little better. That's why we're going to have the award presentation at Van Kemperama."

"My Van Kemperama?" Claire asked. "Can't they have the presentation someplace else?"

"But this would be great for us," he said. "You know there have been some complaints from parents about the kids spending too much time and money at the video games. When they hear about Milton, they'll beg their kids to spend more time and money at Van Kemperama. That's why we've got to make the most of it. Newspapers, radio stations, the works. Milton says it's okay with him. He even gave me the name of someone at the computer company. I'm going to see if they can send a representative."

"Oh, no," Claire said under her breath. If Uncle Horace thought all this news was going to make her feel better, he had another think coming.

"Well, you can't have all the great ideas," he said. "I figure it's my turn."

"It's a great idea," Claire said numbly.

"I'd like to talk to you about some of the details," Uncle Horace said. "I've brought some papers I thought you'd be interested in."

"What papers?"

"We're going to put up a big display in honor of Milton," Uncle Horace said. "He was a little embarrassed by the suggestion, but I put my foot down. So he went home and brought back a lot of his sketches and some of his notes for the display. I guess he's a little shy too. He didn't seem too enthusiastic, but I insisted. I was hoping you'd have time to pick out the ones that would be most interesting. We'll get a big photo of Milton to put up with it."

"Sounds lovely," Claire said.

"I'm glad you think so," Uncle Horace said. "Can I leave them with you?"

"Sure," Claire said. "Anything for Van Kemperama."

Uncle Horace put the papers on the kitchen table. "I knew this would cheer you up."

Before Claire could say anything, Uncle Horace had gone. Milton's papers could wait till tomorrow, she thought. In fact, they could wait forever. As far as she was concerned, working on a display in honor of Milton was the last straw.

But Claire couldn't help looking. She picked up a notebook and looked at the first page.

Video games was written at the top. Claire started to read what she and Van Kemperama had inspired. But it was the handwriting more than the words that caught her eye. There it was, the script of her special valentine. She looked for the funny *o*'s and the uncrossed *t*'s. They were there too. Claire didn't have to compare the handwriting with what was on the valentine and the notes. When she came to the last page of the notebook, a dreadful, heavy feeling took hold of her.

Now Claire understood why Warren had never spoken up. He wasn't her secret admirer any more than Arthur or Greg or Gaylord. Her secret admirer wasn't even a sixth-grader. What was worse, he was the nerdy fifth-grader who had robbed her of her Junior Achievement Award.

Claire's secret admirer was Milton Marango.

Chapter Twelve

Nipping It in the Bud

More than once Claire's mother had told Claire never to drop by someone's house unexpectedly, especially around dinnertime. But that afternoon Claire had no time to waste on niceties. She marched up the walk to the Marangos' house and pressed the door bell. The door opened, and Claire saw Milton's mother peering out from behind it.

"Mrs. Marango?" Claire asked.

"Claire Van Kemp?" Mrs. Marango asked.

"I hope I'm not interrupting your dinner," Claire said. "It's just that I wanted to congratulate Milton."

"How nice of you," Mrs. Marango said as she gestured for Claire to come inside.

"I also wanted to go over some papers for the display at Van Kemperama," Claire said.

"You dear girl," Mrs. Marango said. "Milton

is so happy and excited. I know he'll be thrilled to see you. Let me call him." Mrs. Marango went to the staircase and called, "Milton, dear, come down. There's someone here to see you."

Milton hurried to the top of the stairs. He started down the steps. When he saw Claire, however, he stopped abruptly.

"Claire's come to congratulate you," Mrs. Marango said. "She's brought over the papers for your display at Van Kemperama."

Milton nervously took one cautious step after another down to the last step of the stairway. "Hi, Claire," he said. "You brought my papers?"

"Uncle Horace gave them to me," Claire said. "I'm in charge of setting up the display."

"You two will have to excuse me," Mrs. Marango said. "I have to start our dinner. Thank you, Claire, for stopping by."

Mrs. Marango walked toward the back of the house. Milton stood on the bottom step of the stairway, clinging to the banister. "I was kind of wondering when you'd be getting the papers," he said. "Did you look at them?"

"Certainly," Claire said.

"Well, maybe we can talk about the display some other time," he said. "It was your uncle's idea, you know."

"I know," Claire said. "I think there's something else we should talk about, Milton."

Milton stepped off the bottom step. When he

and Claire were standing on the same level, the top of his head came just to her nose. It put him at what they call a psychological disadvantage.

"Look, Claire," Milton said. "I know you and your uncle want to set up the display as soon as possible. But couldn't we talk about it tomorrow or the next day?"

"I'm not here about the display," Claire said. She opened her briefcase and pulled out the notes and the valentine. "I'm here about these," she said. She held them out to Milton, but he didn't reach for them. "You know what they are, don't you?"

Milton took a step back. "They're just envelopes," he said.

Claire held up one for him. "Don't you recognize the handwriting?"

Milton didn't move. "You're the handwriting expert, Claire," he said.

"I know whose handwriting it is, Milton," she said. "There's no point in denying it. You sent me those notes, didn't you?"

Milton nodded his head slowly.

"Then you admit it," Claire announced. "You're my secret admirer. Really, Milton, how could you do this to me?"

"I had a feeling you wouldn't be pleased," Milton said. "That's why I was your *secret* admirer."

"Just tell me one thing, Milton," she said. "Why?"

"Why?" Milton repeated.

"Why did you do it?"

"Because I admire you, Claire," he said. "Ever since the first day at Van Kemperama. When you were emptying the Moon Patrol game."

"That's not good enough," Claire said.

"But I do admire you," Milton protested. "It was good enough for me."

"The way I unload a Moon Patrol game?" Claire asked.

"It wasn't just that," Milton said. "It's everything about you. The way you think and talk. The way you do things. You're the most admirable person I've ever met in my life."

"People don't send valentines to people just because they admire them," Claire said. "They don't go around sending notes worshiping the ground someone walks on, either."

"But I do worship the ground you walk on," Milton said. "You told me to go invent my own video game, so I did. I'd do anything you told me to."

"That's not admiration," Claire stammered. "That's, well, that's something else."

"I guess I feel something else for you, then," he said. "I'm sorry you're taking this so badly."

"I'm taking it the same way any other girl in

my position would take it," Claire said. "Be reasonable, Milton. Please, be realistic."

"What's my admiring you got to do with being reasonable or realistic?" Milton asked.

"Look at me," Claire commanded. "What do you see?"

"I see someone I worship, adore, and admire," Milton said.

"That's what you think you see," Claire said. "What you see is a sixth-grade girl who was on her way to winning her second Junior Achievement Award until you came along. What I see is a fifth-grader with his head in the clouds."

"What does that have to do with my feelings for you?" Milton asked.

"My point is that I am twelve years old and you are ten," Claire said. "Don't you realize that when I'm sixteen, you'll just be fourteen? And when I'm nineteen, you'll be seventeen?"

"And when you're a hundred and six, I'll be a hundred and four."

"Very good," she said. "I knew you'd understand."

"I understand the addition and subtraction," Milton said, "but I don't get your point. What's a year or two difference in our ages have to do with anything?"

"It means that any feeling between us is impossible. I'm not saying that to hurt you, Milton. I'm saying it to spare you."

"Feeling between us?"

"There isn't a chance that I could feel about you the way you feel toward me," Claire said. "That's what I mean."

"But I wasn't asking you to feel anything for me," he said.

"You say that now, Milton," she said. "But you'll find out that unmutual admiration societies can be very painful. I know what I'm talking about."

"I don't mind."

"Don't beg, Milton."

"I'm not begging."

"Don't cry and plead," Claire said. "Don't do anything desperate. Just accept the fact that I do not feel anything for you and go on with your life. Find some girl in the fifth grade and admire her."

"But I don't admire anyone in the fifth grade the way I admire you," he said.

"Really, Milton," she said. "I'm trying my best to let you down easily, but you're making it very difficult for me."

"It's just hard for me to understand that someone wouldn't want to be admired," Milton said. "Even if it's by me."

"Someday you will," Claire said. "Besides, you said you would do anything I asked you to do."

"That's true," Milton said. "I did say that. I'll try to stop admiring you, if that's what you want."

"It's what I want," Claire said. She picked up her briefcase and glanced at Milton again.

Milton looked up at her sadly. "If I do keep on admiring you, I'll keep it a secret. Even from you, Claire."

"Thanks, Milton," Claire said.

She closed the Marangos' door behind her and walked to the sidewalk. As she walked, she realized that she had said everything she had meant to. Now she could kiss all the secret admirer nonsense good-bye once and for all. That was something to feel good about, wasn't it? Claire could only wonder why she just felt hollow inside—as though she had been robbed twice in one day.

She had lost her Junior Achievement Award, but worse, she had lost her secret admirer too.

Chapter Thirteen

True Confessions

When Claire went to sleep that night, she didn't dream. The next morning she felt disappointed. She had grown fond of her dreams about Warren and looked forward to them. She realized that she would never have one of those dreams again. Now that she knew the bitter truth about Milton, Claire doubted that she would ever dream again.

Claire dressed and went down to breakfast. Her parents were already at the kitchen table.

"Still upset about the award?" her mother asked as she poured Claire a glass of orange juice.

Claire shrugged. Last night she had talked to them about it.

"Does that mean yes?" her father asked.

Claire nodded.

"Would you believe me if I told you that you won't feel so bad forever?"

"Probably not," Claire said. "I have a feeling

that from now on my life is strictly downhill. I guess it's time to let the younger generation take over."

"Really, Claire," her mother said. "You won last year and maybe you'll win next year. Don't let this get you down. Winning isn't everything."

"But I wanted to win two years in a row," Claire said as she rested her half-empty glass on the table. "Maybe I've lost that certain something that made me stand out."

"Don't be too quick to judge yourself, Claire," her father said. "Remember, it's just as bad to underestimate yourself as it is to overestimate yourself. You seem to be doing a bit of both."

"I'm not doing either," Claire said. "I'm being perfectly realistic. I'm a twelve-year-old has-been."

Claire's mother poured warm milk into a cup and added chocolate syrup. "Drink it, dear," she said. "It'll give you strength."

Claire looked her mother in the eye. Although Mrs. Van Kemp wasn't smiling, Claire wondered if she were trying to cheer her up again. She took a sip of her hot chocolate anyway.

There was a knock at the door.

"Who could that be at this hour of the morning?" her father asked.

Claire went to the door. Through the little curtains she saw Warren.

"It's Warren Fingler at this hour of the morning," she said.

"Invite him in," Claire's father said.

Claire opened the door. "Good morning, Warren," she said.

"Hi, Claire," he said as he stepped into the kitchen. "Good morning, Mrs. Van Kemp. Good morning, Mr. Van Kemp."

"What's up?" Claire asked.

"Nothing much," Warren said. "I was just out for my morning constitutional. I wondered if you'd join me."

Claire faltered. Now she had to face the fact that he wasn't her secret admirer. "I'm taking the bus," Claire said. "I don't have time to walk to school."

"Claire," her mother said. "You have plenty of time. The walk would do you good."

It didn't look to Claire as though she had any choice. She collected her briefcase and put on her sweater. She kissed her parents good-bye and followed Warren out the door.

"I didn't know you were still doing morning constitutionals," Claire said.

"I wasn't," he said. "But now that the weather's warmer, I thought it would be a nice thing to start up again."

Claire nodded, but she didn't say anything. She had enough to feel embarrassed about without remembering how she had practically thrown herself at him. They walked two blocks without saying another word.

"I'm sorry about what happened yesterday," Warren said. "You're not too disappointed, are you?"

"Humiliated is more like it," she said. "I thought I had that award in the bag. Who would think that I'd be aced out by a fifth-grader."

"I was once," Warren said. "Last year when you beat me, you were in the fifth grade. I lived, if it's any consolation."

"But you were in the fifth grade too," she said.

"Still," he said. "I'm willing to bet you'll live."

"That's only half of it," Claire said. "You remember all that fuss about the card I got from a secret admirer?"

"Sure," Warren said. "It was the talk of the school for about a week."

"Milton Marango was my secret admirer," Claire said. "Isn't that pathetic?"

"Milton's brilliant," Warren said. "If you don't mind my saying so."

"Well, you see, I sort of thought it was you," Claire said. "When I was doing my Madame Claire Voyante act and you wrote down 'Roses are red,' I thought it was your way of telling me. I guess you meant it when you said it was just a phrase you had picked up in your mother's store after all."

"Is that why you've been so nice to me lately?" he asked. "Because you thought I was your secret admirer?"

"It's pretty silly, isn't it?" Claire asked.

"Maybe," Warren admitted. "Here I was liking you because I thought you liked me, while you were liking me because you thought I liked you. Well, don't worry, you've got plenty of admirers left. You got all those valentines, didn't you?"

"It's not the same," Claire said.

"Only because they weren't secret admirers," he said.

"They weren't for real, Warren. I sent them all myself," she said.

"I didn't know you cared about that sort of thing," he said.

"I didn't know it myself until it was too late," said Claire. "See what I mean by pathetic?"

"Do you like me, Claire?"

"What's that got to do with anything?" she asked. "Here I am about to resign from the human race, and you want to know if I like you."

"Do you?"

"I think you're okay," she said.

"Just okay?"

"Okay, better than okay," she said. "I like you. But don't think I'm boy-crazy, because I'm not. I'm not sure I'll ever have a boyfriend. I just thought it would be kind of nice to have a friend like you, that's all."

"Are you going to send me a valentine next year?" Warren asked. "Or are you going to stick to your old mailing list?"

"I don't think I'll be sending out any more valentines for a very long time," Claire said. "They're not good for my health."

"I'll be sending you one," Warren said. "I figure it'll be good for my interpersonal relationships."

"You mean friendships?"

"I guess you could call them that," he said.

As they approached the steps to the school, he stopped. Claire didn't. She walked up the steps and walked through the main door.

"Claire," he called, but too softly for her to hear him. "Have you heard a single thing I've said?"

Chapter Fourteen

Apology

Claire figured that there were three kinds of people in this world. The first were the kind of people you never notice, even if they are standing right in front of you. The second were the kind of people you notice *only* when they're standing right in front of you. The third were the kind of people you notice even if they're not there. After a little reflection, Claire decided that she fit into the third category, especially when it came to Van Kemperama. If she weren't there two days in a row, people would start asking questions. Kids might even wonder if she were sore about losing the Junior Achievement Award.

There was no way she could avoid Van Kemperama for another day. There was no way, either, that she could get out of preparing the display for Milton. But the one thing she knew she could never do was to go to Milton's award presentation. Claire just didn't have the heart for it.

That afternoon Claire showed up at Van Kemperama, said hello to Shirley and Gaylord, who were playing Moon Patrol, talked to Marcie, made change for Randy, and even played a couple of games of Ms. Pac-Man with Gracie.

By the end of the afternoon she congratulated herself on putting on such a good show. For several seconds she hadn't given the award a single thought. But fifteen minutes before close-up time Milton appeared. When she saw him, all the bad feelings came back. When he walked toward her, the bad feelings got worse.

Claire started to panic. Then, to her relief, she saw some other kids stop Milton. They shook his hand and patted him on the back. As hard as it was for her to see Milton being congratulated, it did give her a chance to escape. She walked into the back room and closed the door behind her.

Hiding in the back room was ridiculous, but Claire resolved to stay there until five thirty. By then everyone would have gone home, including Milton. Someday she would have to speak to him again, but not now, not today.

Claire stood by the sink and watched the clock on the wall tick off the seconds and minutes until it would be safe for her to leave. She groped in the pockets of her jeans for some quarters to wash while she waited. But there were only a few nickels and some pennies in her pockets. There was no point in washing anything smaller than a quarter.

Another minute passed. She heard a knock on the door.

"Come in, Uncle Horace," she called out.

The door opened. There stood Milton. Claire froze.

"Your uncle doesn't knock to come into the back room of his own store, does he?" Milton asked. "Maybe you were just hoping it wasn't me."

"Right on both counts," Claire said. "Look, Milton. I'm sorry I had to hurt your feelings yesterday. I was just trying to let you down easily. I can't talk now. Good-bye."

"I'll go as soon as I say a couple of things to you, Claire," he said.

"If it's about the display, don't worry," Claire said. "It will be ready in a couple of days. Your awards ceremony should be sensational, though I won't be able to attend."

"That's not what I'm here to talk about," Milton said.

"There's nothing to talk about," she said.

"Yes, there is," Milton replied. "I want to thank you and I want to apologize too."

"Okay, but I do have to clean up here," Claire said. She leaned against the counter and waited.

"I want to thank you for telling me to go home and make up a video game of my own," he said. "If you hadn't said it, I wouldn't have done it."

"And I wouldn't be out one Junior Achievement Award," she said.

"That's what I wanted to apologize for," Milton said. "I didn't make up the game to win anything. I did it because it was kind of interesting to do."

Although Milton's words didn't make Claire feel any less miserable, she could tell that he was sincerely sorry about winning. Maybe almost as sorry as Claire was about losing.

"I accept your apology," she said. "I'm sure you really didn't mean to win my award. But I'll tell you one thing, Milton. If I had had any idea that someone in this town could put together a video game and sell it, too, I would have kept it to myself."

"Thank you for listening to me, Claire," Milton said.

"Good-bye, Milton."

"Bye, Claire."

She watched him leave the room. He wasn't such a bad kid, Claire thought. It was just too bad that he was too brilliant for her own good. Claire guessed that she had to learn to keep an eye out for other overachievers. You just couldn't tell who they were going to turn out to be.

Suddenly a *ting* shot through Claire's body. She ran into the video game parlor. No one was there. Not even Milton. Claire ran to the shop door. If Milton had walked to Van Kemperama instead of riding his bike, he couldn't have gone far.

"Milton," Claire yelled as she looked down Main Street. "Milton!" she yelled again as she looked in the opposite direction. There he was, walking by the Five and Ten. "Milton, there's something I want to tell you. Come back!"

As she started to run after him, he turned around. But he didn't come toward her. He just stood where he was until she caught up with him.

"We're not through with our little discussion, Milton," she said. "Not yet."

"You're still mad at me," he said.

"I may be mad at you, Milton," she said, "but I'm not going to bite you."

Claire took hold of Milton's arm and led him back toward the store.

"I didn't expect you to be pleased," Milton said. "I just wanted to explain."

"I'm not mad at you for the reason you think," she said.

"In two minutes you've thought up a whole new reason to be mad at me?" Milton asked.

"Just because I thought up the reason quickly doesn't mean it's not real," Claire said.

"Okay, Claire," he said. "Let me have it."

"I'm mad at you for apologizing," Claire said. "You have no right."

"But you accepted my apology."

"First things first," she said. "How dare you apologize for winning the Junior Achievement Award? You should be very proud of yourself. I didn't apologize last year when I won. You shouldn't apologize, either. Milton, I hereby reject your apology."

"I take it back," he said. "If that's what you want."

"It has nothing to do with what I want," Claire said. "It's just the way things should be. You should be jumping for joy instead of feeling lousy. The award means you're the best."

"It means I made an outstanding contribution," Milton said. "It doesn't mean I'm anything more than I was before."

"That's not the way people around here see it," she said. "Including me."

"I know other people think more of me because I won an award," Milton said. "And I like people thinking I'm special. But an award isn't going to make me feel special unless I feel that way about myself already."

"You always thought you were special?"

"Well, I thought I was okay," Milton said. "I guess I just feel more okay now. Anyway, I'm sorry things didn't work out the way you wanted them to."

"Don't grovel, Milton," Claire said. "Only nerds do that. And you're not a nerd."

Claire walked to the door and watched Milton walk down the street. Then she stepped back into the store to clean up. Looking around, Claire decided that it all could wait until tomorrow. Tonight she was going home to figure out why Milton didn't need an award to know that he was okay.

And why she did.

That night after dinner, Claire opened her desk drawer and looked inside. The valentine and the love notes were gone. So was her list of her most likely secret admirers. She had thrown all that stuff away. Just one scrap of paper remained in a corner of the drawer.

Claire placed it on the desk. It was the list of her own most admirable qualities. She looked at it.

~~INTELLIGENT~~ EXTREMELY INTELLIGENT
HARD-WORKING
~~BEAUTIFUL~~ ATTRACTIVE

Claire crumpled the piece of paper and threw it away. A moment later, however, she retrieved it from the wastebasket and unfolded it on her desk. Did any of those admirable qualities really apply to her? Well, maybe the attractive part, she thought. Definitely the hard-working part. Certainly not the intelligent part, though.

If she were extremely intelligent, or even just plain ordinary intelligent, she wouldn't feel like such an idiot about the award. Claire picked up her pen and crossed out EXTREMELY and INTELLIGENT. Next to the crossed-out words she wrote DUMB.

She looked at the word. Maybe it hadn't been so dumb to want the award. But it had been dumb to want it so badly. Just the way it had been dumb to have wanted her secret admirer to turn out to be Warren.

Claire thought a little more. There were other people in town who didn't think they were okay unless they had some visible proof of it. Probably there were lots of people in the world who felt the same way. All of them could take a lesson from Milton. She sat at her desk and stared at the paper in front of her. Sometimes you just have to believe in yourself.

Then Claire crossed out the word DUMB. Next to it she wrote HUMAN. It wasn't such a bad word. In fact, she didn't mind feeling human. Once she got used to it, she might even start to enjoy the feeling.

When Claire woke up the next morning, she felt almost good again. She had had a dream about the future. Not the way it might be, but the way it would be.

Chapter Fifteen

Her Shining Hour

Van Kemperama wasn't really so big and the population of New Eden wasn't really so small that *everyone* in town was able to fit into the video game parlor the following week for Milton's presentation. Still, it was hard to remember when more people from New Eden had been in the same place at the same time.

In order to make as much room as possible, Uncle Horace pushed all the video games against the walls and installed a small platform at one end of the room. Facing the ramp were a dozen rows of rented chairs. Uncle Horace had even put up streamers along the walls.

The ceremony was set to begin at four o'clock, but by three thirty most of the seats were taken. In the front row, on the left, sat Milton, all dressed up in a blue suit. On either side of him sat his mother and his father.

Next to them sat two men and a woman who represented the Junior Chamber of Commerce, and across the aisle sat the representatives from Utubi who would present Milton with his check for a quarter of a million yen.

Behind them in chairs that Uncle Horace had marked "Press" were reporters from the local newspapers and the radio station, plus two photographers. Behind the press section sat everyone else. By the time four o'clock rolled around, all the seats were taken and a crowd had begun to fill the rest of Van Kemp Hardware. At the last moment Uncle Horace set up a borrowed loudspeaker system so that everyone could hear what was going on, even if they couldn't see it.

Milton looked around nervously. He checked his shoes to see if they were still shining. He asked his mother if she would straighten his tie. He looked at the clock. He turned around to check the crowd.

Just as the second hand on the clock ticked off four, Uncle Horace walked to the little platform and waved his hands for everyone to be quiet. Milton folded his hands on his lap.

"Ladies and gentlemen, boys and girls, members of the press," Uncle Horace said loudly. "Most everyone in New Eden knows Milton Marango, and many people around the country are getting to know about his accomplishment. Since everyone here knows what today is all about, I'm not going to say anything except how proud we all are of him."

Everyone applauded. Uncle Horace raised his hands again and everyone stopped clapping. "Half the people in this town volunteered to present this award," he said, "but the Junior Chamber of Commerce thought it was most fitting for one person in particular to do the honors. Partly because she won last year's Junior Achievement Award, and partly because she's the manager of Van Kemperama, where Milton got the idea for his game. Besides, she didn't exactly volunteer to present the award. She insisted on it."

Everyone started to laugh and applaud at the same time. Then they turned around to see Claire marching down the center aisle. For the first time in recent memory, Claire had given up her jeans and sweater and was all dressed up in a pantsuit. With one hand she clasped Milton's plaque, and with the other hand she waved at everyone. Of all the people in the room, Milton Marango was clapping the hardest.

When Claire reached the platform, she waited for the applause to die down. Holding the plaque with both hands now, she began to speak.

"Even if I did volunteer the loudest," she said, "I'm still proud and happy that the Junior Chamber of Commerce gave me the honor of presenting this year's Junior Achievement Award. Milton, get up here."

Everyone cheered as Milton walked to the platform and stood beside Claire. The photographers stood up to take their picture.

"Milton Marango," Claire said. "For your outstanding work in the field of computer electronics, you are this year's winner of the New Eden Junior Chamber of Commerce's Junior Achievement Award. There's a lot we can all learn from Milton's accomplishment, and there's a lot we can learn from his example too. I know, because I already have. That's why I'm one of Milton's biggest admirers."

As Claire handed the plaque to Milton, the crowd burst into applause once again. Claire put her hand on Milton's shoulder and looked at the audience. At the very far end, behind the last row of chairs, stood Warren. When their eyes met, Warren raised his hand and made the V-for-victory sign.

Although it's immodest to smile too much when you're getting an award, it's perfectly okay to do it when you're presenting one, Claire thought. She let the smile on her face turn into the broadest beam. Then Claire raised her hand toward Warren and made the V sign too.

RATULATIONS MILT